"You're Something Special."

Frank watched her, and his eyes and face were soft and gentle.

Geri just looked at him.

He told her, "I wish—"

She waited.

He continued to look at her in that same soft way.

She asked, "What is it that you…wish?"

He shook his head. He was still and said nothing more.

She asked again, "What exactly are you talking about that you wish?"

So he finally said the truth. "I'd take you away to a private place and make love to you."

"I don't do that sort of thing. I wouldn't until I was safely married."

"You haven't—? At all?" His mouth was open. He couldn't believe what she'd said. She was a virgin? He was boggled.

But he also couldn't get his eyes off her. She truly was something special, and he would do well to be very careful with her.

Dear Reader,

Welcome to Silhouette Desire—where you're guaranteed powerful, passionate and provocative love stories that feature rugged heroes and spirited heroines who experience the full emotional intensity of falling in love!

This October you'll love our new MAN OF THE MONTH title by Barbara Boswell, *Forever Flint*. Opposites attract when a city girl becomes the pregnant bride of a millionaire outdoorsman.

Be sure to "rope in" the next installment of the exciting Desire miniseries TEXAS CATTLEMAN'S CLUB with *Billionaire Bridegroom* by Peggy Moreland. When cattle baron Forrest Cunningham wants to wed childhood friend Becky Sullivan, she puts his love to an unexpected test.

The always-wonderful Jennifer Greene returns to Desire with her magical series HAPPILY EVER AFTER. *Kiss Your Prince Charming* is a modern fairy tale starring an unforgettable "frog prince." In a sexy battle-of-the-sexes tale, Lass Small offers you *The Catch of Texas*. Anne Eames continues her popular miniseries MONTANA MALONES with *The Unknown Malone*. And Sheri WhiteFeather makes her explosive Desire debut with *Warrior's Baby*, a story of surrogate motherhood with a twist.

Next month, you'll really feel the power of the passion when you see our new provocative cover design. Underneath our new covers, you will still find six exhilarating journeys into the seductive world of romance, with a guaranteed happy ending!

Enjoy!

Joan Marlow Golan
Senior Editor, Silhouette Desire

Please address questions and book requests to:
Silhouette Reader Service
U.S.: 3010 Walden Ave., P.O. Box 1325, Buffalo, NY 14269
Canadian: P.O. Box 609, Fort Erie, Ont. L2A 5X3

THE CATCH
OF TEXAS
LASS SMALL

SILHOUETTE *Desire*®
Published by Silhouette Books
America's Publisher of Contemporary Romance

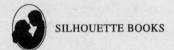 SILHOUETTE BOOKS

ISBN 0-373-76246-1

THE CATCH OF TEXAS

Copyright © 1999 by Lass Small

This edition published by arrangement with Harlequin Books S.A.

® and TM are trademarks of Harlequin Books S.A., used under license.
Trademarks indicated with ® are registered in the United States Patent
and Trademark Office, the Canadian Trade Marks Office and in other
countries.

Visit us at www.romance.net

Printed in U.S.A.

Books by Lass Small

Silhouette Desire

Tangled Web #241
To Meet Again #322
Stolen Day #341
Possibles #356
Intrusive Man #373
To Love Again #397
Blindman's Bluff #413
*Goldilocks and the Behr #437
*Hide and Seek #453
*Red Rover #491
*Odd Man Out #505
*Tagged #534
Contact #548
Wrong Address, Right Place #569
Not Easy #578
The Loner #594
Four Dollars and Fifty-One Cents #613
*No Trespassing Allowed #638
The Molly Q #655
†'Twas the Night #684
*Dominic #697
†A Restless Man #731
†Two Halves #743
†Beware of Widows #755
A Disruptive Influence #775
†Balanced #800
†Tweed #817
†A New Year #830
†I'm Gonna Get You #848
†Salty and Felicia #860
†Lemon #879
†An Obsolete Man #895
A Nuisance #901
Impulse #926
Whatever Comes #963
My House or Yours? #974
A Stranger in Texas #994
The Texas Blue Norther #1027
The Coffeepot Inn #1045
Chancy's Cowboy #1064
How To Win (Back) a Wife #1107
‡Taken by a Texan #1137
‡The Hard-To-Tame Texan #1148
‡The Lone Texan #1165
The Best Husband in Texas #1201
The Catch of Texas #1246

Silhouette Romance

An Irritating Man #444
Snow Bird #521

Silhouette Yours Truly

Not Looking for a Texas Man
The Case of the Lady in
  Apartment 308

Silhouette Books

Silhouette Christmas Stories 1989
"Voice of the Turtles"
Silhouette Spring Fancy 1993
"Chance Encounter"

*Lambert Series
†Fabulous Brown Brothers
‡ The Keepers of Texas

LASS SMALL

finds living on this planet at this time a fascinating experience. People are amazing. She thinks that to be a teller of tales of people, places and things is absolutely marvelous.

One

There's a saying known by its four letters—TGIF or Thank God It's Friday. Well, that isn't exactly what women have in mind. *Their* definition of the quote is: Thank God I'm Female.

Men are slow and think it's another quote entirely. But then, men are different from women.

Now Geri Jones was a normal woman and saw life as it was. At an early age, she was baffled by males. As time went along, she watched them silently. When she matured, she found *all* men are thataway! There *is* no change! Men are strange.

Just try to take a man to a concert when there's a *baseball* game! They go to that.

Their…grandmother…is ill. That's what they say when they leave the office.

It was after Geri was adult that she had TGIF put on her car license plate. She'd looked at males since she was ten, and she had never understood any, nor had she been snared by any one of them.

She searched. The town in TEXAS where Geri lived was big enough. Something over a million people. A good number to paw through and select some interesting males. She was thoughtful, considering, and careful. But few were acceptable. They were generally *not* what she had in mind. So she'd slowly withdrawn. She had just about been positive she'd either have to be a single woman or move away and search somewhere else for a man.

Frank Scheblocki thought Geri Jones was what he wanted. He smiled at her as she walked down the street toward him. He thought just his smile would be plenty and she'd swoon in his arms.

She did not.

Frank was not deterred by her being so difficult. He talked to his buddies about her. There was Tim Slamecki, Jack Smith, Mac Kraft, Mark Goode and Tommy Thompson.

The males discussed the stubborn female who at her age hadn't the guts to smile back. They stood on the street corner and looked at her as she passed.

Geri didn't notice. Not the actual males. They blocked the walk, and *she* had to cope with that stupidity. She walked around them with grim indignation. They laughed. She thought *they* were too old to be thataway.

Frank was trying to catch her eye. He thought she was…wonderful. He wanted her in his house so that when he got home from work, she would be there with all the goodies on the table. The biggest goody being her.

To him, she was special. Frank smiled his hello smile at her. She never noticed. She didn't look at him at all.

Sadly, Frank said to his buddies, "She doesn't like me all that much."

Mark soothed, "She's shy."

Tim agreed. "She's woggled by all us males. Some of us ought to move back and quit looking at her."

"You get back." That was Mark.

Tim shook his head. "I have to stay close to Frank so's he won't bungle the entire encounter."

Mac gasped. "The *entire* encounter." And he put his hand to his chest in shock.

Tommy said, "Cut it out."

"—of the paper?" Mac gasped again.

Tommy groaned and laughed.

It went on thataway. Long past the time that Geri Jones had disappeared. Gotten into her car. Left them. Gone.

The males all noted that she had TGIF on her license plate. They smiled. They were not functioning correctly or they would have known it wasn't Thank God It's Friday but Thank God I'm Female.

That would have boggled the men.

Sometime back, in spite of her mother's tears, Geri had moved from home and gotten an apartment of her own. She lived in a large old apartment house that was back from the river.

When she got home to her apartment after work, she liked the quiet. She took the elevator to the third floor, or she walked it. Whichever she wanted.

She chose which TV programs she wanted and adjusted the sound to suit her. She was tidy. She liked her apartment that way. She'd chosen the third floor because she could see over the TEXAS trees to the river.

Twice a year, Geri had her family there for her mother's birthday and her father's birthday. She was becoming a solid woman. She was twenty-eight. Still single. Alone.

Her parents had given up on her. She would be a single woman all the rest of her life, they grieved. They had discussed her from the time she'd left them.

Geri gave bridge parties now and again. She included men. They liked cards. They visited with the other men. The males paid little attention to the women.

However—

Two of the men thought Geri was a good partner. She worked, she had her own apartment, she had a car, she was very well set financially. They smiled at her and each separately offered to bring the bread and wine for supper—each told her that would be between just him and her.

Geri smiled. She said, "I'll call."

She never did.

Geri went to visit her parents before the drive home. Her mother Ann told her, "You're too picky. Find a man you can endure and get married."

Geri replied, "I'll see."

It was a nothing reply. Her mother was aware of that. It silenced her. She realized Geri probably wouldn't *ever* be interested in

any man. There were women like that. Ann
looked at her husband and thought he wasn't
at all difficult.

When Geri left, her mother saw the TGIF
but then she realized it was different.

That made her mother think for a while.
She said thoughtfully to her husband John, "I
wonder if Geri will *ever* marry."

Her husband lifted his eyebrows without
moving his eyes from the evening paper and
said, "Ummmmm."

Ann looked at her husband and breathed in
indignation. But she said nothing.

Geri drove to her apartment house and
thought about what and who she had to consider seriously. Frank? She thought about him
as she drove into the open garage under her
apartment.

She nodded to people who called to her
without replying vocally. She was lost in
time. She stopped and looked out to the river.
The land between was kept empty of houses
because the river rose and flooded.

If houses were in that area, they would be

a part of the mess. She didn't consider it because her mind was on her own life. What did she want?

And at that time, two cars came along and honked as they stopped. It was Frank Scheblocki and some of his friends.

Frank got out of his car and stood, allowing her to admire his body and his smile. The other guys got out also, but they stayed closer to the cars.

Frank moved slowly to Geri.

Geri sighed silently. There were men who liked concerts and men who studied newspapers and magazines to know what was happening where. But this male saw *her,* and he followed her, and he noticed her. He made her feel special.

She smiled and turned out her hand. "Are all those males along to take care of you?"

Soberly watching her, Frank asked, "Could I come back by myself? Would you mind?"

She looked at him and nodded. "I'll fix you supper."

He grinned. "I'll be back." Frank went

back, calling openly, "In the cars. I've been invited to supper."

Some male gasped, "*You* have?"

And Frank nodded. "Just me!"

As the various males got into their cars, they protested not being invited, too.

Geri slowly shook her head, being sure the rest of the males would not come back, too.

They laughed and protested and called out, but they all left in the two cars.

Geri wondered what she'd done. Well, she could control any male. She'd feed Frank after all, and she'd shoo him out after they'd eaten. If he walked over to her place, or someone came by and dropped him off, she'd call a cab for him when the supper was finished.

So she went inside her apartment to the kitchen and looked at what all was available to eat. Shocked, she saw she had very little. And Frank was coming right back. So she went next door to another apartment and asked her neighbor, Paul Gorden, "May I use some of your goodies? I've asked a young man to have dinner with me. He is willing."

Paul said, "Only if I can share the supper you're preparing."

She laughed. "Do you suppose that there will be enough to eat?"

Paul said, "I'll help. Of course, you'll have to include me for dinner. Not to eat me, you realize, but to feed me also."

She tilted her head and said, "Okay. It's a deal. What all do you have to eat?"

So they searched out what was available. She put the things aside that she wanted. Then she heard Frank's car door slam. And he was walking up the stairs to her apartment!

She told Paul, "I've got to hurry. I didn't realize he could be here so fast."

"I'll bring the other things over. Be sure to set me a place at the very table you're fixing."

"Done." And she grinned as she left.

Geri got to her door as Frank got there, grinning widely and his eyes sparkling with anticipation. That was for food, but Geri thought he was anticipating something romantic—and Paul would be there! She laughed. How hilarious.

Frank thought she was delighted to see him and his grin widened.

Geri looked over at the approaching Paul. Paul was serious and his head was down like a bull's as he watched the intruder.

Now Paul *knew* she was having a guest. What was the matter with him? Geri took a deep breath and looked at Paul with some hostility.

Paul didn't notice. He was watching Frank.

Understanding the males' hostility to each other, Geri sighed and said, "I've a terrible headache. I'm sure you both will excuse me."

That old, tattered excuse came right out of the blue. Think of that.

Frank was startled that he'd taken the time to be there when she'd just discarded him.

Paul told Geri quietly, "I'll see he gets out right away."

She looked at Paul and said, "Thank you. I'll see you around, no doubt." Then she closed the front door.

Paul gasped.

Geri turned and went into the back of the apartment to her bedroom, and she closed that door, too.

All that in just no time at all?

A little while later, Geri came from the back room to check out who was left. Since no one was there, Geri drew a deep breath and hummed as she gathered what was left for her own supper.

The fact that the two men had carried away most of the meal was no problem for her.

As Geri ate, she sat looking out over the beautiful trees to the river. It was a wonderful view. She smiled at the scene, though her thoughts kept returning to Frank.

Time passed. Several days. The phone rang.

Should she or shouldn't she answer the silly thing? Geri wondered.

But she considered that as she got up and went to the phone. She lifted it, not saying anything, and it was Frank who asked, ''You okay?''

"Yeah."

Then Frank asked as if the thought had just occurred, "Hey, you wanna go to a movie?"

Geri asked carefully, "What movie?"

And he said, "*Twilight*. It's supposed to be good."

"I've heard it's scary."

He told her, "Naw. It's just like all the others. You've probably seen 'em on TV. Try this one. I've seen it, and it's okay."

"If you've *seen* it, why are you willing to go?"

And Frank told her, "This way I can watch you and how you take the movie."

"That would be boring for you."

In a smoky voice, he told her, "I can watch you."

That made Geri feel naked. She considered all the other people who'd be there so she'd be okay. She said, "You'll watch the screen. Behave."

Frank complained, "Oh, hell. That again."

"Yeah."

He sighed with such endurance and said, "Okay."

"Well, I'll see if my headache takes care."

Frank exclaimed, "That still around? I thought you were through it."

Geri told him, "It comes and goes... depending." What a lie.

So Frank said, "Maybe you ought to see a doctor?"

"It's the season. I'm one who stops up with colds at summer's tip."

"*Ahhhh.*"

They talked a few moments longer, making plans for the evening. And when Geri hung up, she was oddly warmed by Frank's concern for her.

So that evening, the two did go to the movie, *Twilight.* Geri looked around to see who else was there and did not see one single person she knew. When had that ever happened?

Geri settled down and adjusted to being in a strange place.

The movie *was* odd and caught Geri's attention quite easily. She watched the screen and was drawn into the plot. She felt the people were real, and their problems were just like everybody's! She blinked and listened. She *never* shouted what they could have done! But she was restless and appalled they weren't a little more aware of what all was happening.

When it was finished and they were on their way to her place, she told Frank what the actors should have done right away and not allowed it all to pile up.

Frank said, "It's a movie."

Now that was logical. The film wasn't real. So she settled down and still it waggled in her mind.

Frank told Geri, "You were so wrapped up in what was happening." He grinned at her.

She was more serious. She said, "They *never* should have—"

"It was a movie."

Geri told him, "The plot was such that I could have done better."

"Yeah. Want something to drink? Or how about ice cream?"

"Ice cream. If they'd only—"

Again he repeated, "It was a movie."

She was somewhat irritated. "Aren't you involved? Didn't you figure out what they were supposed to do right away and not let it get all out of hand?"

He laughed, then said, "What you need is a good cherry soda."

"Chocolate."

He was shocked. "You don't want a cherry soda? You're waggling my understanding of you."

"Probably." She was sassy and slid her eyes to look at him. She really wasn't finished with debating the movie. "So you've seen it twice now?"

Frank nodded. "I had to check it out to see if you'd like it."

That touched her. "Thank you." But she was irritated by the film. "It should have gone differently."

"How?"

"The female lead should have been more in charge of the situation."

He nodded. He did that because he wasn't entirely sure exactly what she intended for the characters to do. Frank looked over at her and watched her tilt her head as she looked out the car window into the night's darkness.

She was precious.

He took her to a busy ice-cream place that had sandwiches and beer. They got out of the car and went inside.

"Hey, Frank!" The call was for Frank, but the table of guys were looking at the remarkable Geri. The males got up and joined them at their table so that they could each sit by Geri.

Frank smiled. But he kept a good strong hand on the woman who was with him. He said, "Hush, now. Watch your language. This is a lady."

Two

How interesting it was for Geri Jones to listen to the men speak and tease and laugh. They acted as if they had no other way to spend their time. What did they do?

So she inquired.

Their jobs were odd. She asked, "How did you find them?"

They shrugged and looked at each other. One man painted traffic signs. One was an electrician who strung new wires where they were needed. Another was in construction and altered buildings that were unsound.

All of them adjusted things. They knew how and it wasn't difficult. And they knew how to read the drawings and help in the building of a building.

She asked, "How'd you know to do that?"

Some of them shrugged and one said, "It was logical."

She asked, "How did you know *what* to do?"

It was Mark Goode who listened and replied, "How it was, wasn't working, so we figured how to change it so that it would work."

Geri was amazed. Anyone who could do something like that was clever.

Jack Smith told her, "We have lots of help on such things. There're men who draw and figure and decide."

"Who?" she asked.

"Guys that can figure out why it isn't working. They can be desk people or people who do that kind of thing and knew it was crooked at the time they put it in. Some ideas for buildings are really dumb.''

She watched the speakers seriously and suggested, ''Do any of you ask about things you *know* are wrong?''

''Yeah,'' one of the older men said. ''But the one that designed it doesn't allow us to comment.''

Geri asked, ''So you figure then what you'd have done if you'd drawn the layout?''

''Naw. They could be right. It's when we find they're wrong, and nothing really works right, that we figure how to save it. Some things don't save. They're empty and dead.''

''Ahhhhh,'' she said softly. She was thinking and considering. The apartments where she lived were somewhat that way. Some of the places were without good views. It was almost as if they'd been slapped in place and left that way.

One of the older men told her, ''The place you live?''

Now how did he know where she lived? So she just looked at the man.

Easily he went on, "Some of the apartments were redone. We had to change them. The people who'd moved in didn't understand outside walls that nobody could look out of."

She nodded as she said, *"Ahhhh."*

The older man who was called George said, "We put in the windows."

So she asked, "How about an outside porch?"

George shook his head. "No support below. With the windows, you get to see out. That's as good as we could do."

She laughed. "It's perfect! Thank you."

And another of the men, John, told her, "You should have heard the people complaining because they couldn't see out. That's when we finally got to put in the extra windows."

Geri told him, "It was brilliant. How long ago did they finally agree to allow you all to put in the missing windows?"

"Some years ago. The people that were to move in there objected to not being able to see out the walls. Other people just didn't move in. So the ones in charge of that place called us back. And we charged them double.''

They all laughed.

She smiled at them until they were silent, then she said, ''It was worth it.''

They smiled at her.

With subtle élan, she said, ''They charge me *three* times as much because there are the windows.''

The older man waited for the laughter to soften, then he told her, ''We'll talk to them and straighten them out.''

They all laughed, including her.

The older man looked at her and smiled gently. But he was silent.

She said softly, ''Just having those windows is worth your work.''

He smiled, but he was still silent.

She thought she'd offended him with her laughter.

So it was only three days later that the receptionist of Geri's development called to

Geri as she went by. The woman told Geri, "We are startled because we've been over-charging you for rent!" The woman smiled. "You get a refund."

And the money was counted out and then recounted as Geri was paid!

She gave half of it to Frank and asked that he pass it on to the man who had made the windows.

Frank asked her, "You sure? It's your money. George was paid to cut out those windows. He didn't lose any cash at all."

"But he told me why I was being charged extra. Those windows had been paid for a long time ago by the people who lived there."

"Yeah." Frank was thoughtful. "I'll give him the money again."

"Thank you."

Frank watched her. "I don't understand you all the time."

"I'm a woman. I can roar."

He watched her. His eyes sparkled. He licked his lips. He told her, "You're special."

So Geri went home to find a large basket

of flowers at her door. It was from George. He wrote, "You got dinner coming from me and my wife either Friday or Saturday. Let me know." His phone number was at the bottom.

She called and told the answering machine, "This is Geri. I shall be delighted to take *you* and your wife to dinner. Let me know when. I'll drive."

When the time came, it was Frank who drove to fetch her, and they went to pick up George and his wife, Martha. Geri told Frank, "I hadn't planned to feed you, too. You eat like a horse."

Frank replied, "Horses eat grass and stuff like that. I eat steaks."

"So you're the one who uses up all the money!"

"Yep. Get adjusted."

She laughed. She looked at Frank and watched his smile. She settled down and enjoyed the evening.

George had brought Martha along so that she would do the talking, and he need not.

However, it wasn't long before George broke in and told stories that were really funny, and they all laughed. He was a great storyteller and the stories were simply hilarious.

They ate and laughed until late that night...the four of them. Then they went back to Geri's apartment so that Martha could see out Geri's precious windows facing the river.

It was lovely. They all stood at the windows and looked beyond the tops of the trees to the TEXAS water that moved in the moonlight. It was special. The night was also. The four of them laughed and snacked the tiny little things Geri had put out for them, and they had beer.

There was laughter and hilarious talk that was wickedly off base. The men were astonished the women were amused by such things! The men protested and exclaimed and were so shocked!

The women's amusement caused tears to run. Geri had to find tissues. She shared with Martha and they laughed some more in the exchange. The women were exhausted from all the hilarity and they told the men they had to be serious and cut out the humor!

The men nodded seriously, all concerned, but they slid their eyes to each other. And they told more humorous stories about friends who worked with them

It was late when Frank suggested they take George and Martha to their home. Geri laughed that she would leave her own place to see the others home.

But George said, "Frank'll take us by the place we're working on and let you see where we are."

Geri blinked. It was late. She had to get up early for work. She put on a sweater and went with them down to the car. She had no idea why in the world she had done such a dumb thing! Geri decided it was because Martha was there, and it was the courteous thing to see to it that she got home okay. Yeah.

Geri was amazed at the construction site. George was a genius.

But then George mentioned that it had been *Frank* who figured out how they would fix

some of the amazing things that they had
done in that house. One was a table that could
be collapsed just so. Another was a window
wall that gave the illusion of being outside—
in spite of the wall.

How people figured to do things was an
endless amazement to Geri. So when she and
Frank returned to her house, she commented
on how much she loved looking out the windows.

He smiled at her. She had pleased him.

So, *Frank* had been the one who'd designed her windows. It might have been
George who had put them in, but it had been
Frank who had done most of the work. He
was a doer.

Geri smiled at him.

He reached for her and she gasped and
jumped back. She told him, "Do you know
what time it is?"

"Mine."

"No. I have to get up in the morning and
go to work!"

"I have to be at the place we're now working about seven. Without holding you, I'll be hyper and restless and difficult.''

Standing on the sofa, supposedly out of reach, she tilted her head back and said, ''I shall be worn out and dragging.''

Frank told her, ''Women are strange.''

''Peculiar?''

Frank nodded. ''Different. We're boggled by women.''

So she asked, ''Oh? And just how many women do you know?''

''My mother, my sisters, my cousins. They're all strange and different just like y— all the other women.''

She laughed. He'd slid around blaming her so quickly that it amused her.

He said, ''My God. How am I going to behave and leave you be while I want you against me and in my hands?''

''Control.'' She was logical and then said, ''Hustle up and leave. I've got to get to bed and sleep!''

Frank said, ''Oh.'' He'd thought the bed reasoning was a different thing altogether.

She meant to sleep? Women! How did God *ever* do this to another *man?*

Geri pulled on Frank's sleeve so that he got to the door, and she opened it. He looked at her as if he was a zombie.

She told him, "Good night. Your car is out yonder, right over thataway." She pointed.

He nodded, not paying any attention to her chattering at all.

Geri took his arm and pulled him out the apartment's door, then she stepped back, closed the door and leaned against it as her body went furiously, cruelly berserk.

It was a while before she heard his steps go slowly down the stairs. Was he a zombie or was he thoughtfully careful? The light was on. He could see.

She fought opening the door and looking out to be sure he was all right. If she did that, she'd ruin everything. She'd take him to bed.

And she began to remember all the things her mother had told her before she left home and got her own apartment. Her mother was opposed to her daughter going out to live in an isolated apartment.

Her mom was right.

Geri went to the partial window in her bedroom and looked down into the parking lot.

His car was there. Where was he?

Geri stretched to look around, worried. She was just about ready to run down to see if Frank had tripped when he walked slowly into the moonlight, his hands deep in his pockets.

He was all right. But he moved so slowly! Was he ill? She thought she ought to run down and see if she should take him to the—

He stopped again, pushed his hands down deeper in his pants pockets, as he leaned his head back.

Was he going to howl at the moon? Dogs did it easily. Would he?

She watched. She was different than she'd ever been in all her life. Why should she be interested in Frank. *Would* he howl? How would she respond to that? Would she be shocked? Or would she open the half window and howl back?

Surely not.

Frank stood, looking up at the moon. He had no idea Geri was watching him through a window. Finally he moved and went over to his car. He got into it and sat there as if he didn't have a key.

Geri smiled. He would come ba—

The car's engine started. It throbbed just like her heart. Frank moved the car easily and slowly. He carefully went out of the lot and on down the exit road out of sight by the trees.

He was gone.

He'd been there with her.

She moved her hands on her body. She wished they were his hands. She breathed. She put her hands to her face in agony. She paced. She went into the bathroom and stripped. Then she got into the shower and stood as the water came down on her body. She moved her head. Her hair didn't need water.

She was disgruntled. She was alone. She could have been in bed with him right that minute!

No.

What she needed was a good run, then to go to bed and sleep!

So Geri turned off the shower and got out. She dried herself roughly, then put on her silken red runner outfit. She locked the door as she went out…and she had the key.

That had become automatic. She'd forgotten the keys so many times that she'd taught herself to have one along. She got really ticked with having another made.

The crew wouldn't give her a key. They figured if they gave her one, she'd just lose it. This way, she was more careful. Annoyed, but more careful.

So she ran around the apartments a while in the moonlight and irritated the evening crew who watched what was going on. They mentioned that she ought to go to bed and quit running around that late at night.

So she told them to hush! She had a problem, and she was trying to solve it. She needed them to leave her be!

That scared the liver out of them, and they

had to watch her to be sure she wasn't
snatched or didn't fall and break a leg.

When she called "Good night!" cheer-
fully, they were indignant. She was their
worst person at the place. They *never* knew
what the hell she'd do next. They watched
her, frowning, just waiting for her to go to
her own place.

She did. They communicated by transmit-
ters in their shirt pockets. "She's in her
place."

And the others said a really snide, "Glory
be." They mumbled it in throat-squeezing,
muscle-tight irritation.

Upstairs, in the apartment, Geri stripped
the sweaty, hot, red silk off her body. Then
after she showered again, she crawled into
bed and went right to sleep. To sleep—per-
chance to dream?

Naw. She slept, out cold, a deep sleep.

On her way home the next evening, on her
car phone, Geri called her friends at their of-
fices. They were a tad later leaving than she.

So she asked Margaret Buckman, Marian Terse and Dorothy Oswald to come to dinner that night or the next.

The three said, "Tonight" and hung up. That meant they probably wouldn't bring any food along but expected to be fed. Okay. So she'd do that.

Geri went to the grocery and spoke to all the people who worked there, plus all those shopping. She didn't actually know them all, but her grandfather had been in politics and he always spoke to everybody, and she had the same habit.

It was interesting that some people didn't look up at all, or they looked at the stranger with some startled indignation.

Geri never noticed. She was always in a hurry. That's the way her grandfather had been, and she simply felt the need to speak…as he did. He was very fragile and amused. He smiled always. That was a cheerful thing to do, and so Geri did it, too. It was the way of the family.

Her mother thought it was nice that Geri

copied her grandfather. Geri's daddy thought she was a tad odd. He told his brothers that his daughter was a whole lot like her mother's people.

His brothers nodded. They never said anything. They just agreed.

So Geri went to her apartment with all the goodies for supper. She sorted out things and put some into the oven and some into the refrigerator.

She set the table and had everything ready when her three friends arrived, already caught up in a marvelously complicated discussion in which they included Geri. They all talked and listened and laughed. They washed their hands and settled down to eat.

They told Geri that they'd found a cat on their way over that had been lost. She was skinny and big-eyed. The three women had dogs, so they'd brought the cat to Geri.

Geri looked at the rather tacky animal and frowned. "I'm supposed to keep this creature?"

And the other three were startled that Geri

was surprised. Margaret told Geri. "You're to find a place for the cat."

"Oh."

And it was Marian who said, "Feed her right."

Dorothy commented, "Don't bring in a dog for a while."

Indignant, Geri objected, "I haven't had a dog."

"—yet." All three said it at the same time and laughed.

Geri mentioned, "We're not allowed to have dogs and cats here."

"Well—" they were entirely logical "—see to it that you get her a home right away."

The next day, Geri asked Paul if he knew of anyone who would like a cat.

Paul said, "Give her to the pound. You can tell your friends that she has a good place to be. They'll never know."

Soberly Geri looked at Paul. She listened to his words, said, "Thank you" and left. He called to her but she didn't respond.

She went to see Frank. He was pulling out roots at a job site. He was so pleased to see her. He listened to her tell about the cat. He nodded. "I know an old woman who likes cats. She has a couple. She'll find somebody to take a good cat."

Geri told Frank, "She needs help. She's skinny and has been abandoned."

"I'll fix her up with some food. Don't worry. It's easy." Then he asked, "You okay?"

She smiled. A tear came out of her eye.

He was alarmed. "What's going on? Who's pushing you? Tell me. I can handle it."

"I don't have any problems...now. If you can find the cat a place, you've solved my problem."

He watched her seriously. He said, "I get a kiss."

She tilted her head several times quite sassily and she felt in her pockets. She looked in her purse. She said, "I *had* some kisses ar—"

So he kissed her.

There were cheers and claps and hoo-hahs and guys who hollered, "Me next!"

Nothing seemed to reach Frank, but the guys hollering made Geri laugh and blush scarlet!

Frank told her soberly, "They're young. They don't know about love...yet. They will."

She laughed and blushed some more and said, "Good heavens! You're wicked!" She grinned at those whistling and told Frank, "You're not supposed to kiss me when all those guys are around this way."

Very soberly, he told her, "Okay. I'll save the kiss for later when we're alone. You free for dinner?"

She opened her humongous purse and clawed around until she came out with a book. She opened it and gasped in delight. "I'm free tonight!"

Watching her, Frank warned, "I'm serious."

"About the cat?" She was teasing and her eyes were sparkling.

Very seriously, he told her, "I want you for supper."

She gasped and asked softly so that no one else could hear, "You're going to eat me?"

Slowly he began to smile. He told her, "I'll nibble on you...here and there." His hands indicated her body, but he could have been explaining some house and how it opened and where.

She laughed.

Three

After dinner that night Frank watched Geri and knew she was different from any of the women he'd known. He was wobbled a tad. He told her earnestly, "You scare me."

That baffled her. She became serious and asked, "Why are you scared of me?" She regarded him with concern.

Frank again told her, "You scare me."

That made Geri laugh. She thought he was being subtly funny.

But he didn't laugh. He watched her with concern. As if he wasn't what she wanted.

Geri laughed again. She thought Frank was being sassy and teasing her.

He told her seriously, "We're not in the same boat."

She looked around as if the boat was there, and she was so amused. She asked, "Which boat—where?" And she felt as if she was sharing the hilarity.

He told her, "We're not the same kind."

She sobered. "You think you're ahead of me?" But she didn't wait for a reply. She said, "How foolish of you."

Frank asked, "You think I'm a fool? I probably am. I ought not try for you at all. I ought—"

She frowned and protested, "Frank—"

"Listen. I'm telling you what's happening. I'm a man who wants you, but I don't have the moxie to be with you. I ought to realize that. You're magic and something—"

Geri sighed and told him, "What makes you believe we're not suited for each other?"

Frank watched her seriously. He told her, "I work with my hands. I'm good at what I do, but I don't have the education the other guys have. I could make a good living for us, but if we have ch—"

She replied with her nose up and her eyes serious. "You're an exceptional man who manages to make things work."

Frank shook his head. "I just do the best I can."

She laughed. "How come I hear about you from the other men? They think you're exceptional."

"Exceptional?" He watched her. "You're exceptional. I could use your body and be a part of you for a while. But I love you. I want you to be with me all the rest of our days."

She laughed and reached for him. But he backed away quickly and groaned. He told her, "I want you, but I know it isn't right. I'm a simple man who leads a simple life. I don't know if that will be enough for you. I need to get away from you before it's too late. I never should have tried to be close to you."

"Now what in this world is the matter with you?" She was losing her temper. "Here I find you and want you and am delighted to even see you, and all of the sudden, you want out! Do you have another woman? Answer me this very minute!"

Frank watched her soberly.

Geri waited for his reply.

Frank said, "I need to leave you be."

She watched him in shock.

Frank sighed and repeated, "I never should have gotten close to you. I should have been smarter."

He was releasing her entirely.

"How dare you be calm!" she said. "I'm infuriated with you."

He gasped, then said, "Honey!" His eyes were serious.

She could have walloped him, but she was a lady and ladies simply did not do anything rash that way—but she just might be the odd-ball one who *did* do that! She breathed and considered him seriously.

He watched her. He was earnest.

She tilted back her head as his eyes slid down her body. She asked, "Did I forget to put on some of my clothing?"

And he told her, "No." He came slowly to her, his eyes looking at all of her, and his seriousness was completely charming. How rude.

He gathered her to him and just held her against him softly. He told her, "I love you." And he held her to him as if he loved her— and she loved him?

She gasped in air and moved her mouth to object—

He kissed her! He did! How dare he do that to her at such a time. She was woggled. She was not in control.

He held her close to him and said softly, "I want you, so I'm willing to take the risk. I'll be here for you until you find the man you want."

That popped open her eyes. He was holding her so close, she could not step back. And it would be rude to push him away when he was so careful with her.

She cleared her throat and looked up at his jaw with indignant indignation.

His eyes were closed so he didn't see her indignation, and he was hugging her and groaning.

He was groaning with want at a time like that when she was appalled with his conduct?

Geri told him, "I would be shattered with the intrusion of a friend when I'm sure you will apologize. I'll lock the door—if you'll release me."

He picked her up in his arms and went to the door. He waited. He asked, "Wanna lock the door? My hands are busy."

Without anything said, she locked the door.

He carried her into the bedroom. He looked around. He told her, "This is neat."

She looked around and thought the place was a trifle sloppy. He was just being kind? Making up with her?

He kissed her again. She had to lift her mouth and tilt back her head, but she had helped. And the kiss was worth whatever it cost her.

Was he going to make love with her? What did he have in mind? She'd never been intimate with a man. He was— He was—

Her breathing changed and was loud! She was excited. She wasn't being normal at all. She gasped.

Frank asked her, "You okay?"

"Yes."

"You sure you're okay?"

"I have no idea."

Frank began to smile. His eyes were wide and surprised, but the smile was quite good. He told her, "You want me?"

"I've never shivered like this without it being cold. I have no idea what's the matter with me."

Frank smiled and his eyes actually danced! They did! And he said, "You wicked woman."

She was indignant. She told him, "I haven't done anything, as yet."

That "as yet" was wicked as all get out. She heard herself say that! She was startled by her conduct, but she was so interested in what might happen, she didn't move one muscle! She waited for him to do something.

He held her close to him and he laughed so softly. Geri had no idea what all could take place. She had never done anything that would so closely connect a female to a male!

Her eyes moved quickly and her breathing was rather heavy, but still she didn't move! She rested her body against his standing one. She was in his arms and just waited to see what might happen.

What would she do?

She had no idea.

Right on cue, the doorbell rang.

Now who would do something like that? If they were quiet—

Frank said, "Want me to go see who it is?"

And to her shock, she nodded! Now what in the world would make a woman do a stupid thing like that? She was perfectly capable of going to her own door herself!

Geri tried to maintain some balance. She used her hands to be sure her face was normal. And she put her fingers through her hair in a way that made it wild.

She did that.

She didn't notice that she did. She was not paying close attention to anything!

Frank watched her soberly.

Now why did he seem like a lost child?

He moved his hands on her body and leaned her against the wall as he called, "I'm coming!"

What did he mean by that? Geri's eyes got big and her breathing changed as she watched him very seriously.

Frank leaned over and kissed her gently on her cheek, then he breathed very seriously and put his hands into his trouser pockets. He looked at her, then he walked stiffly down the hall and to the front door.

Boneless, Geri leaned against the wall and tried to sort out what all had taken place and just what sort of woman she was!

Tommy Thompson's voice came through the opened door. He said, "Well, hello! What're you doing here?"

She couldn't quite make out the low comment from Frank.

Tommy asked, "Is anybody else here?"

No reply was spoken, but Frank must have shaken his head as he waited for the intruder to leave.

Tommy laughed and said, "You poor man. All alone!"

She listened carefully.

Tommy said, "I'll just settle down until she's ready to chat."

God only knows what Frank did. But he did something, because Tommy laughed again in that way of men.

That made Geri curious. She pushed away from the wall and suddenly began swaying. Her feet didn't seem to understand what they were supposed to do!

While she sorted all that out, she heard other comments from the men at the door. But she didn't process the comments through her brain. She was concentrating on making her feet move.

How come her feet had that problem? They

never had acted so stupid before that very day! Why now?

How come Frank could just go ahead and walk down the hall to the door? How'd he do that?

Having witnessed Frank doing exactly that, and not being able to do it herself, simply irritated the socks off her.

She heard the front door close with some dispatch, so she figured Frank had gone off with Tommy. She'd heard a male laugh and the door had closed.

So Frank had left her and—

Frank appeared silently and stood in front of her. His eyes were intense. Why were they so intense? She was amazed at his regard on her! So she looked at Frank.

He thought she was looking at him in want and he was supposed to do something rash. What if she was hostile about sex at that minute? But she was watching him and she didn't say anything.

When women watch thataway and don't talk at all, Frank knew from experience, they expect a man to take over and hold them close and kiss them seriously. Males find that out at age twelve and watch to see when budding women do that so obviously. Geri wanted him. He could tell.

He approached her gently.

She told him, "My feet are off course."

She was serious.

He looked down at her feet, and they looked okay to him. He looked up at her face. She was serious and watching him very somberly.

She wondered what Frank had said to Tommy that had made him leave.

Geri said to Frank, "Who was that?"

For her to ask that was startling to Frank. She knew who was there. Why would she pretend not to know?

Frank said, "It was Tommy."

"Oh?"

"I told him to run along."

"Why?" She was blank-eyed as she asked that.

Frank told her, "I wanted you to myself."

She asked soberly, ''Alone?''

He looked down at her. ''Yeah.''

She said, ''Let's go into the living room.''

He was very adult about being startled because he didn't show that he was shocked by her. He was in control. He waited.

She watched him.

He was somewhat boggled to realize that she was not really in control—*he* was in control of *her!* He smiled a tad. He waited, not wanting to hustle her along. She was a flower. He had to be careful.

She pointed down to her feet. She needed him to adjust her manner of walking and get her started. Otherwise, she'd probably fall right on her face.

Frank looked down at Geri's feet, and he mentioned, ''You wear neat shoes.''

That comment slid around in her brain. *Neat shoes.* She'd never heard any man mention shoes to a woman at all! She looked up at Frank and considered him.

Frank thought she wore neat shoes. She looked at her shoes. They were…shoes. Nothing unusual. What was he actually watching as he looked down at her?

It was not shoes.

She told Frank, "I need your arm for just a minute."

That boggled him. She wanted him to touch her? Okay.

She told Frank, "I need to see if I can walk by myself."

Now that did shock Frank. He gasped. He did! And his eyes were wide and vulnerable. She could see past his black lashes. She saw his eyes!

They were blue.

She smiled. She licked her lips. That was to let him know she was in control.

Of course, her stupid feet still didn't know which way to go.

She frowned just the tiniest tad and looked at Frank. He didn't do anything! She said, "Help me walk two steps. My feet—"

Slowly Frank began to smile. He knew she wanted to keep him.

She took two steps.

Having taken two steps and finding she could do that, Geri lifted her chin and looked at Frank. Frank was extremely amused by her boggle. He appeared to believe that women were vulnerable. How foolish.

Geri said, "Take care."

Of what? Frank wondered. He reached for her, but she moved her shoulders and kept her hands close to her so that he couldn't grab her. And she went and opened the door.

There were two men there. Frank's friends, Tim and Mac. Both were delighted they'd found Geri at home. They looked past her to Frank.

They nodded with interest and their conduct was a little stiffened. Watching Frank, the two men asked Geri, "You okay?"

And she retorted with some élan, "I'm fine. Good night." She said that to Frank.

Frank was surprised. He asked, "You okay now?"

And she told him, "Yes."

Frank looked at the two men. "You want something?" That he said quite hostilely and a shade possessively.

Geri gave Frank "the look" as she told Tim and Mac, "He's leaving. Come inside and visit a while."

That irritated Frank, but it put controlled hilarity into both Tim and Mac. Frank said, "I've not had any beer."

Geri sighed, then simply turned and led the way into the living room, which overlooked the treetops and gave the guests the wide, marvelous view of the river beyond. It was dark, but the lights on the boats and the streetlights all helped people see what was there. Even without the lights, the moon or just the stars would have allowed the watchers to see what was beyond.

With some hostility, the three men sat and watched each other. Of course, Tim and Mac were extremely amused and had to cough to cover the hilarity that rolled over them.

Both Geri and Frank ignored the sliding glances the two men exchanged. It was not a funny situation for Frank and Geri, who were deadly silent. But it was hilarious for Tim and Mac.

The two men looked out the windows, across the treetops to the river, and they chatted with animation. Geri made comments. Frank did not. He looked at the two guests with a hostile watch that was endless. These men knew of his interest in Geri, yet here they were, having just shown up at her apartment.

Both Tim and Mac seemed amused by Geri and Frank's discomfort. They saw it immediately, and they stayed deliberately because of it. Neither Tim nor Mac was involved so they could be amused. They stayed, cheerful, watching, exchanging quick, hilarious looks.

And they stayed even longer.

Frank was of the opinion that Geri was a victim of the intruders. So he was there to protect a lady who was alone.

Geri was tired and irritated and she wanted them all to leave as soon as they could. It seemed to her that Frank had no reason to stay, but she could not tell him to run along.

How timelessly they all sat. And talked. And laughed. They drank her beer. She never allowed any of them to believe she had any more.

Geri watched the men and listened. Slowly she began to understand their amusement. She began to smile just a tad.

Unfortunately, it took Frank a whole lot longer. He was hostile to men just a tad older than she who flirted and laughed and teased…with her.

Frank needed to feel that he was important to her. He didn't want any other males around to try for her.

That knowledge made Geri's smile even broader.

Four

———

Geri rose and said, "It's late. It's time for you two voyagers to leave."

And one asked, "What about him?"

That irritated the hell out of Frank.

She tilted her head and replied, "He's my guest."

"Your guest!"

Geri raised her eyebrows and held Frank's steel arm in place as she said, "I invited him. You two just walked over without any invitation.'' Now as softly said as that was, it was harsh.

The two guests, a little shocked, rose carefully, expecting her to laugh and tell them to sit still.

She said nothing but watched with a tilted head, waiting for Tim and Mac to leave.

By then she'd moved next to Frank and she'd slid her hand along his arm. She hadn't looked at Frank, she'd only calmly, silently watched Tim and Mac.

What Geri did was her own doing. She had never asked or waited for any comment. She did as she wanted. She was in charge. It was her life. She had always done things her way.

So Tim and Mac left Geri and Frank. In leaving, the two guests looked at each other and smiled. They said not one word to either Geri or Frank. Not until they got to another friend's house. Then the two spoke easily and craftily about Geri and Frank.

''Who's Frank?'' That was said endlessly! But by the time the evening was over, and the crowd had mostly split up to go other places, there were those who had heard of Geri being with Frank Scheblocki.

And men say it is *women* who gossip. Hah! They say that it is women who tell tales. But it is only men who give out actual comments.

Probably everyone in that area of TEXAS knew about Geri and—for Pete's sake—Frank Scheblocki. Those hearing for the first time gasped and pulled back their heads in startled surprise.

Of course, while Frank Scheblocki was single, he was not what the women wanted for Geri. They discussed that every time they got together, just about. The subject always turned up. They decided Geri was not for such a man. She should be kind and release him.

That was probably logical. Why would he want to be around any such woman? They discussed that. They decided they would take Frank into their own hands and show him what it would be like for such a man to be involved with a woman so far up in the echelon.

They then argued and got hot over who
was going to be The Woman. They tightened
lips and flared their eyes at each other in hostility.

There were women present who fought
their hilarity. They slid their eyes over to
other women who were like them.

However, the intruding women were unable to decide what they ought to do with
Frank. Instead, they talked about his eyes and
his grin—and his body.

With the day about gone, Frank came to
Geri's house from work. Despite how they'd
left things recently, he had to see her. He carried his humped lunch box his mother packed
for him.

Geri smiled at him as she opened the door.
Then she saw the lunch box. And she did remember that he was rarely anywhere that he
could go someplace to lunch. He opened the
lunch box and ate what his mother sent.
Knowing that, Geri smiled at Frank.

He grinned as if she was something perfect
and he held her to him.

She looked up at him with her chin on his chest and she asked, ''How'd you get so freshly washed with changed clothing this fast?''

''I take these clothes with me and shower before I get here. That way I smell better.''

She was sassy. She said, ''Oh? I'll just see.'' Then she put her hands on his arms and she leaned forward.

And he kissed her.

He was breathing rapidly. She told him, ''You didn't give me time to check you out.''

''Go ahead.''

She laughed. She tilted her head, and she was kissed again. She blushed with her pleasure and waited for another kiss.

But Frank's head went back and he groaned. He told her, ''You put me through a meat grinder.''

''I do not!'' She laughed. She asked him, ''How'd you get here so quickly? I just got here.''

He considered without letting go of her. He told her, ''I had to shower and change my clothes, so I was quick.''

"How could you have been quick when you showered and changed your clothes?"

"There's a shower on the first floor where we're working. I got first dibs on it. Being first helps."

"How?"

Very seriously, Frank told her, "I don't have to yell at the guy singing in the shower."

"What do they sing?"

"I'll never tell...."

And she laughed. She told him, "You need some females around there."

Frank replied, "We have some. They don't use the shower because we're there first and lined up naked. And if they come along to share the shower, they're disgusted with us. They go home."

"Now why should the women be disgusted?"

So Frank replied, "We are naked and we talk and hoot and misbehave."

Geri laughed. She blushed red, but she did laugh.

Frank said not one thing, but he smiled as he watched her avidly, and he bit his lip as he grinned.

Geri watched him and her grin faded. She said, ''You come here now and you're shined up and wearing clean clothes. How long will that last?''

''Do you mean how long before I sweat over you and smell different? Or do you wonder how long you can love me?''

She nodded for the last one.

He said, ''Until I die.''

She put her arms around him and laid her head against his chest. She told him, ''I love you.''

''When did you finally decide?''

''I suppose it was the first time I saw you and it just happened.''

''Maybe. We'll see.''

She tilted her head back and watched him, then she asked, ''Why will we see?''

''For some reason, people don't always meld. Sometimes people seem to be hooked, but they aren't. They see another mate and leave the first person. You could do that.''

"Or you could."

"No. You're what I want. I don't want to look around or hunt any further. You're perfect."

She sighed, a big, tolerant inhale, which she exhaled as loudly. She said, "You're blind. I'm not perfect."

"To me, you're perfect."

"For now. I'm different. You're fascinated—"

"Right."

She told him, "Hush. You're fascinated for a while because—hush—I'm different than the women you've known. Be quiet. Those women are excellent, but you're bored by them at this time. You will change."

Frank asked gently, "Because you will be bored by me?"

"No. Men look around. They change their minds, become bored, find another woman who is different—younger."

Frank shook his head. "That's not the way my people are. We're for life."

She asked, "But is it something shared? Or

is it locked in and the couple is unable to escape?''

He shrugged. "I only know the people I know. They're kind and gentle people. I don't know about the people you're used to."

Geri looked at Frank with some indignation. She said, "I have good friends."

Gently he told her again, "I don't know about the people you know."

He was so kind that Geri reconsidered the people she knew. There were people who had flaws. She considered the ones who had no flaws and she was bored by them.

Geri then remembered other people who chose to be aloof, who chose to select those friends they could endure.

But there were people whom others chose and endured and laughed over. They were human. What they did was what they wanted. They were individuals.

Geri looked at Frank and asked, "What do you endure?" She'd just thrown it out rather hostile.

He grinned and told her, "I have a grandmother who calls me by my dad's name. She doesn't realize he's grown up and older now. She believes he's my age and it's me she chides and quarrels with. My dad nods and agrees with her!''

Geri laughed softly. "My father's mother chides *him*. He is patient and kind to his mother."

"Why?"

"Oh, I expect he'll get to that age, and he'll be difficult just like his mother."

Frank considered. "Why don't we move far away and write notes to them."

She nodded. "That's tempting."

Frank shook his head. "I would miss seeing them. I'd miss the others, too."

She sighed. "I understand. At least I'm out of the house."

So Frank inquired, "Do you miss being home?"

"No."

Frank laughed. Then he asked with interest, "What is it that made you move out?"

"I'm not sure." Geri considered. Then she

went on, "They had the usual comments to make and then I had to clean the house. I found that a real nuisance."

Frank could see that. "My mother is very dear, although she complains a whole lot about what we ought to do. But even if we do it, she redoes it. She never quits." He looked at her. "Doesn't this all catch your interest? Don't you long to meet my mother and dad and see the others?"

"I see you."

Frank laughed. "That means that I ought to be comforted by the fact that I live at home?"

"It astounds me that you're living at home."

"I get to take care of my parents, and I never have to do anything at all in the house. Mama won't let me."

She considered. "You'd probably do that to a wife. She could be a slave. You'd be a guest in the house."

"Yeah. That about tells the whole story." Frank laughed.

Geri asked, "What else does your mother do?"

"Cards. Shopping…for *her*. The garden. Bridge. Her friends. She never quits."

Thoughtfully Geri shared, "I like all her distractions."

"She's a hell-er. She wants the house just like it ought to be. One book or one shirt out of place and you hear about it fully."

Geri grinned. "You ought to put them away right away!"

"Yes, ma'am."

"I'll accept that reply."

Frank told her, "Come with me for dinner. You ought to meet my family."

"I'll look forward to it. Will the food be perfect?"

In shock, he said, "What a picky female you are!"

She lifted her eyebrows and said, "Of course."

That just made him laugh.

So Frank arranged a night when everybody would be home to welcome the woman he was bringing. His family was wild with curiosity. In preparation they cleaned and even painted one room!

Frank kept saying, "She's just a female."

But the others all said, "They're the ones who check out everything!"

His mother had even insisted his dad get a new mattress for their bed.

Frank's dad complained, "She'll never even notice!"

His mother retorted, "I'll sleep."

His dad raised his eyebrows and asked his wife, "You don't sleep?"

"I know where I am and on what part of the mattress."

So her husband inquired, "With a new mattress, you'll think you're roaming and gone from here!"

That was followed by all sorts of comments and laughter.

Their mother waited, then she said, "It'll be interesting."

Frank was the one who'd spread the news that Geri was going to be a guest at his house.

That brought on an entire collapse of people who wanted to see who she was.

The extended Scheblocki family wanted to be there. Frank's mom told the others to forget it. This was family. The others could see the woman later—if she survived that long.

So they asked, "Why wouldn't she survive? Is she that fragile?"

Mrs. Scheblocki said, "As much as I know about her. Frank tells me she's fragile. But I have to see her first."

Frank loved it all.

It took three weeks before the Scheblockis actually met with Geri Jones.

Geri had looked everywhere for some sort of gift that wasn't too large or too small. She was baffled. Then she'd finally taken flowers.

Mrs. Scheblocki was charmed by the flowers. She even teared up. She smiled and smiled and smiled. And there was that tear that wanted to leap out and run down her cheek, but she would not allow that.

Everybody talked at the table. They all talked to Geri. They laughed. It was so light and easy. And Geri could have kicked herself for being so scared and changing clothes how many times?

Geri laughed until she was worn-out. She could hardly smile as Frank finally took her home.

He told her, "You were perfect."

She shook her head and told him, "It was your family. They are so welcoming."

Frank never countered her saying that. But he did mention several times how kind his family was to her.

She told Frank, "Thank you. But I know they're that way with all the people you all have around. What other female did you take home?"

And Frank told her, "You're the first."

She smiled until her cheeks hurt even worse.

Five

Frank felt lucky to be so close to Geri. They were spending a lot of time together and once again he'd brought her home with him to attend a small gathering. She was magic.

He questioned Geri, "Do you know you're magic?"

She tilted back her head and replied, "Since birth. Everyone accepted that I was… unique." She batted those eyelashes of hers with such innocence.

He nodded seriously.

She laughed in humorous delight.

He told her, "You *are* magic."

She scoffed, "Balderdash!"

So he gasped in indignation and asked, "Now where in this world did you find such a comment?"

As serious as she gasped, she had the audacity to laugh. Her eyes danced and the look in them was naughty. She was wicked!

He licked his lips as he watched his feet move easily, then he lifted his head to look at her. He told Geri, "You need a man to handle you."

"Oh," she commented. She looked around. She moved her head and stretched her neck. She told Frank, "Shucks, there's no one arou—"

"I'll—" he sighed "—see to you." He was so kind!

She laughed.

Now a woman being dealt with by a man thataway ought to be smart enough not to laugh! She did.

That caused a reaction in Frank that he could not smooth out. He looked at her, sighed and slid his hands into the pockets of his trousers.

Meanwhile, Frank's parents were watching the couple.

His father laughed deep in his throat. He told Geri, "Everybody's looking at you."

Geri lowered her head in acceptance of the news, but she was amused.

Frank never left her side. Other men were away from their women, but Frank was close to Geri every minute. He was afraid she'd be whisked away by some idiot. So he held her hand until they filled their plates with food from the buffet.

The food was remarkable. Geri told the Scheblockis, "You're going to spoil us all, and we'll all be on the porch tomorrow, waiting for more marvelous food."

No one had ever told Mrs. Scheblocki how remarkable the food was. Some of her female friends had been kind and said she'd done "a nice job of it," but no one had said it was marvelous. Tears came into each of Mrs. Scheblocki's eyes.

Geri was sobered and asked, "Are you all right?"

"Nobody has ever said my food was marvelous."

Geri leaned closer and told Mrs. Scheblocki, "They're jealous. They don't know how you manage. They eat and they're cross because they aren't as good as you."

Great tears came from Mrs. Scheblocki's eyes. She said, "No one has ever said anything so kind to me."

Geri nodded seriously. "They wonder how you're so clever. I'm a lousy cook and know it, so I can tell you how perfect you are. You do a remarkable job of it."

Frank was shocked. "How come you said that? Now she'll feel like a queen and all her bits and bites are perfect!"

Geri lifted her shoulders to shrug and said, "I was being honest. She is perfect."

His mother beamed, but all the other people frowned at Geri and scolded her. They thought she ought to be smart enough to leave Mrs. Scheblocki alone.

Geri laughed and her eyes caught Mrs. Scheblocki watching her with a smile, her eyes still filled with tears. Geri asked softly, "What's wrong?"

Mrs. Scheblocki told Geri, "You are superb! You have the guts to say what's true. Everybody else shrugs their shoulders and pull their mouths down as they chew. Nobody ever tells me my food is excellent. Thank you."

Geri nodded and explained again, "Jealous."

Mrs. Scheblocki asked, "Do you believe that?"

"I've tasted your magic. They're afraid you'll go high hat and ignore them all."

Mrs. Scheblocki frowned and asked, "How'd you know that?"

"I have a very similar mother. She watches them gobble the food all down and they sigh and say it wasn't too bad."

And Mrs. Scheblocki nodded and said, "*Ahhh.*"

Geri said softly, just to Frank's mother, "Believe me, they're jealous."

A little smile began on Mrs. Scheblocki's face. She looked around the whole place and saw them all eating and talking, but their eyes were on what they were lifting from the plates and gobbling down.

"See?" Geri asked.

"*Ahhhhh,*" said the remarkable woman.

Geri suggested, "Try this dish. I've saved some. It is perfect. You get one third of it. That's all."

Frank's mother laughed softly. She said, "You may keep that. I have some carefully put away."

"Good!" Geri smiled in triumph. "I'll cherish it."

"So. You're the one who's captured my Frank's heart."

"I'm not so sure. I'm a tad different than the females he's used to. He believes I'm out of hand."

"Good. Give him a tough time."

His mother said that! Geri laughed. She

told Frank's mother, "I'll keep you in touch."

Frank's mother tilted her head and said, "We'll see if he behaves and pays attention."

Geri laughed.

And it was then that Frank asked, "What's so funny?"

Geri replied instantly, "Your mother has an excellent humor."

Frank was sober-faced and careful as he watched his mother, but he asked Geri, "What'd she say?"

Geri told him easily, "It was woman talk. It wouldn't be of any interest to you."

That woggled Frank. He looked at Geri in shock.

His mother told him, "Dry up and blow away."

Geri responded with laughter and told the woman, "He's all there is!"

But his mother told Geri, "Be sure." Then she walked away through the crowd and was gone. Just like that. Frank looked at Geri and asked, "What was my mother telling you?"

Geri stood with her chin lifted and her eyes amused as she considered Frank. She told him, "I'm thinking about being serious with you. She told me to be careful because you're dangerous."

Stark-faced and appalled, Frank said, "I am not!"

Geri laughed softly. She watched a disturbed Frank. She told him, "You're very interesting."

Frank asked immediately, "What do you mean by that?"

She tilted her head as she considered, then she said, "I find you are very different than most of the men."

That rattled the hell out of him. He was woggled. He breathed oddly. He was not in control, but he acted as if he was. He watched her. He listened. He was anxious that she had been rattled and would leave him. He told her, "Don't pay any attention to anybody else. Just ask me." He put his thumb to his chest. He watched her soberly and with an intensity that was wobbling for her.

She smiled.

He saw the smile, but he saw the slide of tears from her eyes. He asked her earnestly and almost silently, "Who said what to you?"

She replied, "I believe I love you."

"Only now?" He was shocked. "I thought you loved me—"

"I have, but the love has gotten solid."

"You scare the hell out of me."

"Why?" She was concerned.

He told her, "I don't know you well enough to understand you entirely. I'm really rattled."

She considered him briefly, then told him, "Well, we'll just give you some room and you can decide?" She turned and walked away.

With irritation, he ran after her and stopped her progress. "Are you giving me problems?"

"Without any doubt at all. Leave me alone."

He told her with some patience, "I'm try-

ing to soothe you. Why are you being so difficult?''

Her eyes widened and she told him, ''Release my arm.''

Now what was a man supposed to do at a
time like that with a woman like her? He released her very slowly as he tried to think of
something to say that would soothe her
enough, but his own endurance was nil.

Men tend to be thataway. They want things
done their way. It was a hell of a mess if a
woman chose her way.

Frank watched Geri. She smiled and said,
''How nice to've seen you. Bye.'' And she
turned to leave.

Frank grabbed Geri's hand and held it
tightly as he said, ''Where are you going?''

Frank's possessive hold irritated the liver
out of her. She said with hardly moving her
lips, ''Let go of me...right this minute.''

Frank did loosen his grip and raised his
other hand to smooth her arm. He asked her,
''What is the matter with you?''

She replied, ''I rattle you? You tell me you

love me, then you say you don't understand me. How do you think that makes me feel? Please release me. Leave me alone.''

Frank was shocked and irritated. He told her, ''Behave.''

Well, that wasn't the thing he was supposed to say at that time. Men make odd choices. He could have said, ''Oh, I'm sorry!'' Or he could have said, ''I beg your pardon'' or something like that, but he chose very oddly and it irritated the very liver out of Geri.

Any man knows better than to irritate the liver out of any woman. Men are smarter than that. Well, if they think at all, they are.

Geri looked at Frank and told him, ''Release my arm.''

She said that very clearly, and she startled him quite profoundly. He let go of her.

She walked off from him and went outside. He knew she wouldn't get anywhere because he'd driven her to his home. Suddenly a car stopped and a man reached over and opened the car door!

Frank hollered, "Hey!"

But Geri said something quickly as she got into the car and the male drove away.

Who the hell had that guy been?

Frank drove to Geri's apartment, and he looked into the windows. She was there. Some nut had taken her right on home! He watched her through the window from his car. She walked around busily. She went into the bedroom. He heard the shower. He waited.

The lights went out. He thought that was shocking and gasped. Frank got out of the car and went to her door. He knocked.

There was no reply.

He knocked again. Nothing happened. So he went to security and asked the guy in charge to call her. He gave the man her name and number. The man looked tolerant and kind as he called the number. She answered. The man asked, "Do you want to talk to Frank Scheblocki?"

Even Frank heard her in the silence. She said, "No." And she hung up her phone.

So the man looked with some interest at

Frank. He said, "She must be tired. She hung up."

Frank nodded. "Thanks for trying."

The guy nodded.

Frank told him, "We had a quarrel. I suspect she's going to make me sweat for a while."

The man nodded again. "Women do that. Good luck."

"It's going to be a long night."

"If you're smart, you'll send her some flowers tomorrow very early."

Slowly Frank began to smile. "You've done this?"

"I heard one man who did it, and I've mentioned it to just about every other man around, and it works!"

Unfortunately, Frank's delivered bouquet was pitched out the kitchen window down onto the ground.

Stress makes sleeping nil. Not being able to sleep irritated the liver out of Frank. For days, he moved as if he was a zombie. He was, actually. He called Geri on the phone several times. She did not lift the phone.

Then the phone operator mentioned the number had been changed to a private number. The woman said she could not give out that number and was sorry. She ended by saying, ''I'll tell her you called and give her your number.''

''It's—''

''I have it. It's on the screen when you call here.''

Nothing was sacred. His number was public. Geri's was not.

The operator called Frank back and said sadly, ''The woman does not want a phone call. Thank you, anyway.''

After another sleepless night, Frank called in to his crew and told them his uncle was sick and he'd been up with the man all night. Frank would take the evening slot at the place they were working. They said that would be okay.

Frank was sundered. He'd been positive that he could lure Geri back to him. He had pushed the wrong females away all his life. Geri was right for him. How come she was being so obstinate?

Women!

He tossed and worried and was annoyed and useless and irritated and scared right out of his skin.

He took some aspirin and finally slept and dreamed he was running after...something. He couldn't see what it was. Was it Geri?

She was unique and perfect. How could he convince her that they would be perfect together?

Frank went to work that evening. He was odd-looking in that he'd hardly had any sleep at all, and he was restless and concerned about something else...not the work they were doing.

Frank knew most of the guys. They'd shifted around so many times that knowing them was easy. He nodded and worked. He didn't join in on any of the hilarity or chatter. He didn't tease anyone or give them trouble because they couldn't keep up. He was kind and gentle, and he instructed one youngster in what he was supposed to be doing.

Everybody else was irritated. The young one was the object of their hilarity. But Frank gave the kid good directions. It annoyed the rest of the crew.

Frank told them to behave.

That was about all Frank did to the crew. He told them to hush. He helped the new one and he hushed up the others.

They finally frowned and said to one other, ''Something's wrong with Frank. What's the matter?''

One of the men contacted Frank's mother! She didn't know anything at all and was shocked and upset!

Everybody got upset. People talked and rang the Scheblockis' doorbell and phoned to find out what all was going on. And who was to blame. And what were they supposed to do?

Frank was really irritated by the gossip at first, then he realized his friends and family were backing him and trying to find out what in this world was the matter with him.

Frank told them, "Hush." He told them, "Don't worry about it." He said, "I'll fix it." He said, "Be quiet!" He got mad and said other things.

The women were shocked and gasped. The men laughed.

Some men slapped his shoulder and told him worse things that somebody else had survived. They told it all as something hilarious.

Frank listened soberly. He didn't flinch or laugh or swat anybody. He just allowed them to talk it out, and they were all sure they were the ones who had helped.

Frank didn't say one word.

They all thought he was okay. His mother was wiser. She knew. She was gentle and kind to him. She phoned Geri who was at work. She left a message for Geri to contact Frank.

Well, then Geri came home and listened to all the messages on the phone as she stripped off her office clothes and put on shorts and a top to run in.

There on the phone was a message from

Frank's mother! Who ever heard of a mother calling a woman about a man? That boggled Geri clear to her hair ends. She was to *call* Mrs. Scheblocki and discuss her son? She would not!

So she called Mrs. Scheblocki to tell her that she would not call.

Mrs. Scheblocki answered the phone with, "I was hoping you'd call. I have no idea at all what in the world to do about my son. Do you have any ideas at all?"

Now what was Geri supposed to do? She replied, "I have no idea at all. He is so strange. Where did you get him?"

And Mrs. Scheblocki replied, "God only knows. What am I to do to help this poor, lost person? He's a full-scale irritation. We have no idea in this world what to do with him."

With some testiness, Geri asked, "Can you shift him off onto another family?"

There was some silence, then Mrs. Scheblocki replied, "That's a good thought. We'll try that." And without saying anything else, the woman just hung up!

So the next day, Geri had to call Mrs. Scheblocki to find out what she'd done and if she'd been successful.

Mrs. Scheblocki sighed heavily and told Geri, "I'm trying. He's difficult as all hell."

That rattled Geri somewhat so she asked, "What's he doing?"

"He mopes. He drags around grieving for you. He's driving us all crazy."

"He would. You ought to throw a pail of water on him."

"Why that's what I ought to do! Good for you. Any other ideas?"

Geri told his mother, "I'll write them out and call you."

And Frank's mother replied, "How kind! Thank you."

So the two women exchanged comments and decisions and talked just about every day.

Frank was not aware.

Six

It is something to have someone else aware of what is going on in your life. So when his phone rang and Frank was immediately there, it wasn't Geri who was on the line. It was some woman who was positive she knew what to do about Frank's relationship with Geri. She made it clear to Frank that all he had to do was what she suggested, so he was to listen.

But she was a stranger. Nevertheless, Frank listened and was kind.

The line of calls was heart-filling for Frank. People called him and gave him courage. They prodded him about what he planned to do…and how soon.

So many people had involved themselves in Frank's business, each positive she or he knew what exactly to do. And they gave that knowledge to Frank.

However, it just didn't work out.

Frank found that out just about right away. Now why, he wondered, would any woman close off a man's way of getting to her? Why couldn't he just go over to her apartment and knock on her door and ask what she was up to?

Well, maybe that was what a man did to another man. A woman was more of a problem for anybody alive, but it was especially difficult for a man to understand a woman.

And Frank had no idea at all that his mother and his ex-woman were plotting and chatting. Who would have expected something like that to happen?

Geri continued to call Mrs. Scheblocki, and

they talked about what Geri was doing or should do. And that led to a discussion of TGIF, which Geri told Mrs. Scheblocki, wasn't Thank God It's Friday, but Thank God I'm Female.

Mrs. Scheblocki hadn't heard of that, and she thought it was brilliant! She gasped and laughed and was very animated. She told Geri, "I have to tell this to several people. I'll call you back, but it'll probably be late."

"Whenever."

"That's wise," the older woman told Geri. She added, "I'll be in touch." And she was gone. Just like that. The phone was dead in Geri's ear.

That made Geri feel abandoned. There was no set time when she would hear from Mrs. Scheblocki again.

But her phone did ring. Friends asked what was happening. They'd heard she was housebound.

Geri shook her head at the phone as she told them she was all right. She was loose and free! She was independent. She could just do as she chose! She was able to live and let live.

That made Geri lift her head and look around. She was free! She was on her own. But she was also lonely.

She missed Frank.

And that was when Frank opened Geri's front door all the way. It had been ajar. He watched her earnestly. He was awkward and didn't seem to know what to say. Finally he smiled just a tad and said, "Are you okay?"

She told him openly, "I'm free."

He misunderstood. He asked, "Now? You're available?"

"I'm...free."

So Frank guessed, "To go...with me?"

"I'll consider it."

He blinked, his expression hopeful.

Geri smiled and moved toward him.

That was when her fragile hose caught on a splinter of wood. Geri was shocked and appalled. The blasted hose were too fragile.

Frank got down on his haunches and worked to release her fragile hose.

Geri watched in shock, as Frank handled the snag carefully. She was grateful that he would help her. Hose cost a fortune.

Geri told him, "You do this very well." She slid her eyes over to his face.

Frank didn't even look at her, he was so involved with the caught stocking. He told her, "Such fragile stockings need perfect care."

Geri said, "You are trained well."

"Not in stockings. I've watched a couple of times with my older sisters, but I never saved any like this. You ought to learn to handle this by yourself. Your hands are probably better at it than mine."

Geri thought what a pill he was. She said, "Let me. I can try."

He went on as if she hadn't interrupted, "I think I can save this."

She said, "Never mind. I'll do it." Then she looked at him, expecting him to protest.

And darned if Frank didn't get out of her way! He moved his hands off her leg, and he stepped back to watch.

Geri said, "Move."

He said with raised eyebrows, "I need to watch so I can do the next woman's stockings."

She said, "How kind."

He smiled.

He would.

Geri's head came down like a bull's. Frank was interested. She was *female*. How could she mock a bull? He asked her, "How'd you get that done?"

And she said tightly, "Practice."

He nodded with interest and smiled. Was the smile real, or was he amused? Men are so sly, women never know.

With exquisite care, Geri managed to save the stocking from the catch. She got it free and there was the slightest hole but no run in the stocking. She put some spit on a finger and fixed the drawn, fragile thread.

Frank smiled at her as if she'd done something really important. Then he took her into his arms and held her. "You're so clever. I admire you."

She wasn't sure what he was actually referring to. So she was silent.

Frank pulled his head back and said, "This calls for a supper on me. I invite you to dine with me." He stepped back and bowed.

Geri was startled. She asked, "The drive-in?"

"No…" he said thoughtfully, looking off and considering. "I believe I'll take you to an elegant place and admire your hose."

She laughed. She had no choice. He was actually clever.

Frank smiled. He waited for her laughter to settle, then he said, "How about going to *Occways*. Are you hungry enough? I can't have you pushing things around on your plate."

"I'm hungry."

"Then I should be a good host. If you're really hungry, you'll eat."

Geri watched him with some consideration as to what he had in mind. She said, "I shiver to consider what sort of food you might decide on for us."

"I'll allow you to advise me."

She told him, "I'll do that."

"I'll call so that they save us a table."

Geri nodded. "Good thinking."

So Frank did just that.

*   *   *

It was interesting for them to go to supper the way they did. Frank took them to various places, as if a snack was enough wherever. It was different to go from one place to another and to eat only a selection of things at each place.

It was amusing.

Frank had called ahead, so each place had been ready with whatever Frank had suggested. It was well done, and it took them all evening.

Geri had never before done anything like it, and she was charmed. She wore his flowers…given to her at the first place. It was a small corsage. How clever of him.

They talked. It was very nice. They really enjoyed the visit, the food, the movings to other places. And Geri was charmed by the greetings at the places they went to and the food they were served at discreet tables.

It never was much food, but it was different. And with the gap between places, they weren't filled with the food of any one place.

So Frank asked her, "Is this the way you

like to eat? Here and there? Or do you prefer just one place?''

''Both.'' She lifted her eyebrows and mentioned, ''But I like different things. To eat and move is one way that is perfect, but so is dining at just one place.''

Frank nodded. ''We'll try that next time.''

So they were going to be okay. He was interested enough to say something about seeing each other again. Geri watched Frank and decided she could be with him. She asked Frank, ''How did you get us in at those places so soon? You didn't have reservations.''

''I know those guys. They're nice to me.''

She smiled and nodded. ''You're sly.''

And he admitted, ''Sometimes.''

It was interesting to her that he had contacts in odd places. Not that he wouldn't. He was curious and easygoing. He knew exactly what to do when, yet he had forgotten to hold her chair. She mentioned it.

Frank remembered and laughed. He told her, ''You're spoiled.''

She was indignant. She lifted her chin and said, ''I'm precious.''

His eyes danced. He watched her.

As they drove along home to his house, she asked, "What are you doing for me next?"

"Nude swimming at—hush—a place where there is no one else."

She gasped and then laughed.

He watched her and waited.

So she asked, "Where is that?"

"In our backyard, at night, with no lights. I'll show you."

"I'll contact your mother."

He nodded. "She'll gasp just exactly like you've done in such shock."

"But she'll allow us to skinny-dip?"

Frank sighed enduringly. He told Geri, "I'll have to bribe her. My father will be in the back window with the telescope."

Geri gasped. "Surely not."

Frank laughed and his eyes sparkled like no other man's. He liked her. That was obvious. Was she serious enough to allow his liking? Serious enough to consider him as a husband and father of her children?

She watched and listened to him once they

arrived at his home. He was arguing with the family dog who wanted the entire backyard swing.

Frank put the dog off the swing, but the dog kept his paws on the swing. The dog made no noises at all, but he held his territory.

Geri laughed softly, watching.

Earnestly Frank picked her up and sat her on the swing next to the damned dog. And Frank swung the swing and sang softly to— her? The dog? Which one?

So she asked Frank.

He told her, ''Hush. The dog thinks he's in charge. I'll convince him he's won half of the swing. He'll curl up a little sick from being swung so much. Then I'll move him off and we'll have the swing.''

Geri just laughed softly so that she wouldn't waken his parents.

But Frank's parents were already splitting open windows, watching the couple with the dog out on the swing.

Frank was aware of his parents' watching. He didn't mind. He was being very careful of the woman with him. She was precious to him.

He was not only careful with her, but he was also entertaining her. He made no demands. He was a gentleman.

It had been a marvelous, strange evening. The night was dark and silent. They weren't yet ready to call an end to the evening.

Frank wondered if he would ever be a part of Geri. Would she crawl into his bed? Well, not there at home, of course.

Would *she* suggest that he sleep with her? He tilted back his head and controlled his breaths. He was standing behind the swing, pushing it for her...and the dog.

She laughed softly, leaning forward and back to make the swing go higher. She told him softly, "Get on the other swing and I'll race you."

"I'll watch you."

His sex was rigid and he couldn't sit on a swing or pump one as easily. He could help her swing, though. He could touch her. He could stand in back of her and watch her. His eyes were like a wolf's at night. He could see everything.

And he knew damned good and well that his parents were still watching from the windows silently.

By then, it was after 2:00 a.m. Neither of the couple was yet sleepy.

Frank smiled. He watched Geri in the swing. The dog was spread out and pretending to sleep. But if they watched, the dog opened an eye and watched them. The dog thought no one saw him. Hah!

After a while, Frank walked Geri around to the front of the house, and he put her back into the car. His parents moved, so did all the neighbors who could see. All those darkened houses, and Frank knew good and well the people were up and watching.

He looked at Geri. She was so precious. How could he take her to her apartment and leave her? Why didn't she just take off that nothing gown and get into his bed?

He had to breathe. He was not subtle.

She looked at him and asked, ''Does the summer night rattle your breathing?''

He said, "Yeah."

"Then you need to go inside. Oh, yes, we have your car. Shall I bring it by in the morning?"

Frank said, "No. I'll take you to your apartment first."

She sighed as she smiled. "This has been a special night."

"The food was good."

She laughed. "I was thinking of all the things we did, the places we went. You made the evening very different. When can we do it again?"

Frank asked, "Now?"

She laughed. "I'm so full, I need to walk home."

"Not tonight."

She nodded. "You can follow me in the car."

He nodded. "Or I can pull up the car's floor and you can put your feet down on the pavement and run along inside the car."

"That doesn't appeal at all."

So he said, "Darn! I thought I'd solved it all!"

Geri said, "It's time for me to get back to my place. I shouldn't have made the evening so long. But, Frank, it was perfect."

"So are you."

She laughed softly. She told him, "If it comes to who is better, you are. I've never had such a night. Thank you. You had everything fixed exactly right."

So he asked, "In which of the five places did you enjoy the food most?"

She considered. She said, "That's very difficult. It was all good. Each chef was a genius. No question."

"I'll tell them that."

"Let's practice several times with their food and not say anything, but then we can question them as to what's in it?"

He frowned. "I had no idea you could be so wicked."

She shrugged. "If you tell people that they're perfect, they'll decline."

He gasped, "Is that so?"

"I've watched. You have to be very careful so that people are not swayed away from what they believe is correct."

Frank said, *"Ahhhh"* for whatever that meant. He asked her, "Would you like to take the dog with us and go around the block?"

"You're trying to get me to go home and stop this perfect ni—"

"We'll do as you choose. I swear it. I want you to be pleased."

She sighed. "You'll ruin me."

"In what way?"

"I'll become directive, and I'll want everything my way, and you'll see to it that's so."

"Okay."

She shook her head. "No, no, no. No woman should have the direction on her side. She'll be nasty and ruined."

"Heavens to Betsy!"

She laughed. "You're easy."

"You're perfect."

"Hush," she scolded. "You know better than that. I can't allow any man to believe I'm perfect. I'll be rotten and difficult."

"Okay."

She laughed.

He told her, "It's time for you to get some sleep before tomorrow comes too quickly."

''I know. I've been avoiding it. You're special. How many people have mentioned that to you?''

''Nobody.''

She smiled, pleased down to her very toes that she had been the first.

Seven

It took a while for Geri to understand that Frank was reluctant to allow her to go to her apartment and get into bed...alone, of course. How charming of him to take her to his home so innocently. He could not seduce her—not with his parents there. She knew that. But he could not let her go away from him, either.

She licked her lips and controlled her smile. She looked around. She avoided looking at the windows where she knew his parents were watching them. She also knew they were capable of really rattling their son with their attention.

Did Frank know they were watching? Was that why he hadn't grabbed her and held her and kissed her?

Of course.

But he had her at a safe place where he could watch her. He wasn't driving and glancing at her on occasion. Frank had her where he could watch her and think about her without having to cope with any driving or finding a parking place. Frank had her there, with him!

Geri gasped, "Do you know what *time* it is? I need to go home and get to bed!"

"I'll help—"

She looked at him with such a comment.

He said, "I'll get you home on time."

She laughed. "I believe it's past the time of getting there. I'm lucky I don't live at home. My parents would be pacing! What about your parents?"

He said, "They're asleep."

Yeah. Sure. They were standing back from the windows watching avidly the two who were out of the car and hushfully talking and laughing in the starlight. The sun would be coming up! Even Geri knew that. She told Frank, "It's time for me to go to bed."

Frank said, "We'll sneak up the stairs to my room, and you can sleep while I watch."

Silently Geri laughed.

He told her, "I'm a perfect watcher."

"I'll bet."

He shook his head slowly and told her, "I'll show you how kind I am with a person who needs sleep. I'll see to it that you get to rest."

They were both aware that he was having trouble considering taking care of her in a bed of his.

She told Frank, "Your parents live here."

"They'll stay out of the way."

She laughed softly and shook her head.

So he said, "You think my parents will intrude on a guest?"

She shook her head again and told him,

"You would not possibly rattle your parents with such a guest?"

"They'll adjust."

Geri just shook her head.

"You're of past time. You don't realize how different parents are now."

"I have parents."

Frank was earnest. "They're old-fashioned."

She laughed. Not out loud. Then she was silent. He was watching, there in the starlight, so he saw that she was very amused. And he realized not for the first time that she was indeed special.

He wondered if his parents realized the same thing. Would they know? He was curious to see how they were reacting, over there, back from the windows at the house.

It would be interesting if he found out his parents realized what a golden woman she was. Would they? He'd see.

How interesting that a man in his thirties had parents he wasn't sure about. Would they be as he thought? He found he was observing the house and thinking of them.

Did they know that? They could see that he was looking at the house. Could they also realize he was thinking of them? In what way? Did they think he was interested in this golden woman and wished them away? Or that he wanted them to see her and the way she was? Which?

It was special to be with Geri. She was so different from any other woman he'd met. He remembered the first time he saw her and how zonked he'd been just looking at her.

How had Frank ever managed to get a date with Geri? He knew other women considered him a catch, but what was it that Geri saw in him?

She still scared the dickens out of him. She made him wobble and breathe oddly. He was always expecting her to say, ''Run along'' as she flipped a hand and left him for good.

She was with him now.

Geri said, ''Your parents are especially fine people. The checkers weren't as sure about you.'' She laughed softly.

So he asked her, ''What do you think about me?''

"I like being with you."

"I'm not a guy that's like you. My family and I are different from you and your people."

"I'm a female."

He grinned and bit his lip to control his laughter. He told her, "I'd noticed you are female."

"Well, at least you understand that! I'm female and I like you."

Frank watched her. He told her, "Don't wobble me."

"Now why would my saying that I like you enough to go wherever it is that you take me wobble you?"

"Just looking at you wobbles me. I adore you."

She grinned. "You're supposed to."

"How come?"

"I've decided it." She straightened for a quarrel. She told him, "You're supposed to adore me."

"Yeah."

"Well, if you understand that you're supposed to adore me, what do you mean by the 'yeah?'"

He was very serious. He told her, "I love you."

She told him. "It's too soon for you to decide you love me. You haven't found out any flaws—"

"You got a couple."

She was indignant. "Just what do you mean that I have a couple of flaws?"

"Everybody does."

She demanded, "Just what flaws have you discovered?"

"Well," he said thoughtfully, "Mary slurps and Genev—"

"*Me!*" She raised her chin.

He considered and replied, "Oh. You're okay."

"How tactful." She was ready to go home. She walked toward the car.

He was shocked. "Where're you going?"

"I will not endure a man who is tolerant."

He laughed.

She stopped and turned to see what he thought was so humorous.

And he said, "You're something special." He watched her and his eyes and face were soft and gentle.

She just looked at him.

He told her, "I wish—"

She waited.

He continued to look at her in that same soft way.

She asked, "What is it that you...wish?"

He shook his head. He was still and said nothing more.

Men can be very irritating. She asked, "What exactly are you talking about that you wish?"

So he said the truth. "I'd take you away to a private place and make love to you."

She shook her head and began to walk to the car again. She told him, "I don't do that sort of thing at all, and I wouldn't until I was safely married."

"You haven't—? At all?"

"Of course not!" She was irritated.

His mouth was open. He couldn't believe what she'd said!

She couldn't believe he was that unknowing. Who in this world did he believe she was? She said, "I have never been careless with a male. No matter what he does, I've managed to get away or to call for help. Mostly I've managed to be with other people. Men tend to be very odd." She looked right at him. He was odd.

Yeah. He was. He couldn't get his eyes off her. She was a virgin? At her age? He was boggled.

She told him, "Run along. Your mother's called you."

"I'll take you home."

"I'll walk."

"Not across town. It's not safe."

"Neither are you!"

"I'm pure. I wouldn't touch you now, no matter what you demanded."

"Hah!" And she walked to his car and stood…waiting.

Frank was moving slowly, because he was trying to figure out what in this world he was to do about this very difficult woman. There had to be some way for him to smooth things out and get Geri back to being herself.

He looked at her. There was a large tear hanging on the bottom of one of her eyelashes.

My God…a tear! How could he have done that? Frank said, "Honey—"

Geri lifted her nose and said, "I'll walk. It's only about a mile."

"I'll drive you home."

"Never mind."

Frank said, "Be quiet. Do as I say."

"See? That's just exactly what men say! I will not!"

"Look. I'm going to drive you to your apartment. I'll see to it that nothing corners you. I'll get you there safe and sound." Frank's tone was compassionate. "Honey—"

Geri was furious. She said, "Hush! I'll walk."

"Here we go again. If you walk home, I'll have to drive alongside you and see to it that you get home okay. It will be quicker if I just take you home!"

Frank's mouth was tense. He could grind his teeth. His hands were clenched by his sides.

Geri tilted her head as she observed his conduct. He was being difficult.

Women never are.

Well, her friend Patty was susceptible. Patty was a tagalong who no one actually wanted with them. She was different.

That made Geri look at Frank in a different way. He was not Patty. He was a male. Men are *never* understandable. They live in a world of their own and communicate in a way only they understand.

Frank told her, "Get in the car."

That wobbled her. Just like that, she was supposed to hop into his car and go home? No way. She told him, "I'll walk."

With tight lips Frank said solidly, "Get in the car."

She was shocked, and put her hand to her bosom and gasped, "I'm to get into your automobile?"

"That's what I said. Get in my car."

"Isn't this one your daddy's?"

"It's family."

Geri commented with slightly lifted eyebrows, "I've been in cars that are like this."

So Frank said, "Then you'll know how to do it." And he looked at her with a sober face.

She laughed.

He was ticked.

She walked around the car, looking at it for scrapes or bends. She said, "It's been well kept."

He told her, "We use our handkerchiefs if we see any dust."

She laughed.

He turned his head slowly so that he looked at the car, then his eyes slid back and looked at her.

She tilted her head as she asked, "What name does the family have for this car?"

"The boat."

She shook her head as she considered that. "No. That isn't what you all ought to say. Let's see. The Coach?" She looked at him.

He was finished with her. He was being excessively tolerant in waiting for her to get into the car so that he could take her home.

Frank's brother pulled onto the driveway big enough for extra vehicles. He grinned and asked Geri, "Want a ride? This is a good car. Better than Frank's."

Frank looked at his younger brother in an unkind manner, his eyes scrunched into really mean slits.

John said, "Whoops! Quarrel?"

Geri told John, "He's being difficult, so I'm going to walk home."

Frank said, "Be quiet."

Geri told John, "He means me."

John told Geri very calmly and with some hostility, "I'll take you home. He won't interfere."

She said, "Ah, but he will when you get back."

"I'll sleep at my uncle's."

Frank said, "Hush. Go to bed."

John tilted his head and asked Geri, "You hear that? Do you suppose he's hostile to me?"

Geri told Frank's younger brother, "Don't push him. I'll handle him."

About that time, their daddy walked out like a man looking at the stars. He was probably pushed out of the house by his wife who told him, "Go settle that and get her home!"

Frank asked his daddy, "Why did you come out here?"

"My yard."

That made John laugh. It was deep in his chest and his eyes danced. He was enjoying his intrusion on the lovers.

John said to his daddy, "Having trouble sleeping? Need a ride in a good car?"

His daddy smiled and said, "Your mamma's calling you."

John nodded and exclaimed, "Is she now? I'll put the car away."

His daddy said, "You go do that."

"Yes, sir." It was said so charmingly. But he was right on the edge of laughter. How shocking!

Geri asked the daddy, "Would it be all right if John took me home? He has to move his car anyway."

The boy's daddy said, "Uh-hump."

Frank said to his brother, "Who asked you?" in a deadly challenge.

That was interesting to John who straightened and opened his mouth, but Geri told him, "Hush."

John's mouth opened to explain, but then his daddy said, "Hush."

So John held out his arms so that his hands were up and empty. He shrugged his shoulders and said, "I'm being told like a child!" And he was so amazed and so appalled that he was fake as all get out.

Geri laughed. "You're exceptionally good. Do you appear in any of the plays?"

John bit his lower lip as he smiled, and he coughed once. He said, "I'm working—uh—on it."

Frank told his brother in a very serious voice, "Go inside the house."

Now, Frank didn't say that to his daddy—he was smarter than that—but he could get rid of his brother if he wanted to.

John said to Geri, "If I leave, will you be all right?"

His daddy said, "Go on into the house—*now*."

That was clear enough. John smiled at his daddy, then he said to Geri with a slight bow, "I've been replaced. It's late. I work tomorrow. So I leave you all with my regards. Good night." He grinned, bowed again and backed a couple of steps so that he could turn and go into the house.

The three left were as silent as those watching from inside the houses around the neighborhood.

Frank's daddy told his son, "Take her home so's everybody around here can get to sleep." He turned to Geri, "Good night, honey." And he left. He went into his house and nothing was heard. Not his wife, or John or any of the other kids.

All was silent.

Frank said, "I'll take you home now."

Geri said, "You brought me here, you ought to get me back home again. If you do that, I'll not ask you again to take me anywhere."

Frank told her, "We need to talk. I suppose tonight isn't the time."

"I'm very tired."

Frank told her kindly, "I'll take you home."

She looked at the cars. "Your brother has you blocked."

"He left his keys in the car. I'll take you in his."

"All the people at the apartment house will suppose I have several dates in one night. This car is different."

"You could have a slew of men. Didn't you notice my brother? He was eager to help you out of here."

She said kindly, "He's darling."

Frank frowned and looked at her as he said, "Well, hell."

Geri told Frank, "So are you, sometimes. Not tonight."

Frank told her seriously, "I brought you here because I knew you'd be safe. Anyplace else, along the street or in the parking lot, you have to pay attention."

She commented, "It's startling to realize no one is exactly safe."

"Most are. They're careful."

She looked around. "Like coming here?"

Frank nodded.

"Your brother is a nice person. Hush! And your daddy was shoved out here by your mother? He didn't want to be here."

Frank smiled a tad. His eyes didn't laugh, but his smile was there. He told her, "I have a good family."

"Yes, you do."

"Are you discarding me and taking up with my brother?"

Geri told him soberly, "I like you. Even annoyed and irritated by you, I still like you."

So Frank asked seriously, "Why do you find me annoying and irritating?"

"You are different. I expect you to allow me all the ways I want. Then you tell me not to do this or not to do that."

Frank told her very seriously, "That's to save your neck."

She put her hands on her neck. "It's fragile

and very important to me. I believe I'll listen to what you've said.''

Frank grinned and pulled her against him. He told her, ''I'll always take care of you...if you'll let me.''

Finally, they got into his brother's car and backed out of the driveway. Frank said, ''This automobile is testy.''

That was all he said. So she asked, ''What are you saying?''

''This car is reckless and overloaded.''

So she said, ''Let me drive.''

Frank looked at her quickly to see if she was serious, then he looked back to where the flighty car planned to go. He told her, ''Not *this* car.''

That annoyed the liver out of Geri. She wasn't one to be put aside over a silly idea that the car was different.

When they got to her place, she said, ''Hang on to the bucking car, I'll manage. Good night!'' She kissed his quickly turned, surprised mouth, then she opened the door and dashed off to climb the stairs to the third floor.

Eight

Frank was stunned. He hadn't had the chance to hold Geri's body against his. He got out of the car and walked to the apartment house. He lifted his head and watched as Geri went up the stairs. She was alone. He followed her, taking the stairs two at a time.

Suddenly she was nowhere in sight! He knew where her place was—on the third floor—but he didn't know where she was! He got excited. He knocked on her door.

And she opened the door! He said, "What the hell are you doing opening the door when you don't know who is—"

"I looked through the glass hole, which we have—" she showed him "—and I checked to see who was pounding on my door at this hour of the night."

Frank told her seriously, "I wanted to be sure you got into your place okay."

"I'd have yelled."

She didn't step back and allow him to enter. That made him suddenly aware that she was blocking him. He asked, "Should I come in and check all the closets and under the beds?"

Geri laughed softly and told Frank, "All is well. Go home. Be careful driving your brother's car."

Frank nodded. His face was serious. He told her, "I've never before driven a car like John's. I think when I start back, I'll get out of the car and run alongside and reach in to move the steering wheel."

She laughed. He'd been serious and concerned. Now he smiled a tad.

Frank hesitated. He wanted her. In her bed. He lived at home. She had her own place. She was blocking his entry.

He told her, ''Sure you don't want me to give the place a good look over so's you can sleep easy?''

''It's tick-o-locked and secure. The people who run this place are very careful of us.'' Frank turned and looked out over the trees to the river beyond. ''You got a good place. You can see a long way.''

It was interesting to her that he actually mentioned *her*. Generally men say things about themselves. But Frank saw it all. She understood that he felt close to her, and he did not want to leave her. She knew that.

Frank watched the trees and looked at the sky. He was using time. He wanted her. He breathed as if he'd run up the stairs. Well, he had. But it hadn't been the stairs that caused his breathing to become odd.

Geri was all right. Frank was sure. But he didn't want to leave her. They were a pair. She was his. It had taken his damn brother to underline that for him.

Frank watched Geri. If she told him to go inside with her—hell, he had John's car! He said, "I need to take John's car home. Are you okay?"

She smiled. She laughed softly. "This is a safe place. Did you see the crew as you came up?"

He was startled. He said, "No."

She told him, "There are security crews around and about who know who is here and who isn't. They're very careful."

"Nobody saw me."

"Oh, yes. They called me and asked if I wanted to see you…as you came up the stairs behind me."

Frank was shocked. "They did it that fast?"

"They do it all the time." She shrugged at Frank's amazement. "They're always around."

"Are they watching me now?"

She laughed. "More than likely."

He turned and looked around. "I don't see them."

"Over there." She pointed. "And—there. It's dark, but he'll wave."

And the man did wave once.

Frank said, "So they watch you."

"All of us."

"Good." He was satisfied.

She laughed softly. "Just saying that will make them love you."

"I don't want them to love me, I want them to watch out for you!"

"They do. They really like doing this and it's a challenge for them. It's as if they are plotting a revenge!"

Frank squinted his eyes. "A revenge?"

"Something like that."

"I adore you."

She smiled. "I suspected."

"I've got to see to it that no other man gets around you at all."

She lifted her eyebrows and inquired, "I'm not allowed to speak to other men?"

He nodded carefully, his face serious.

"I do talk to all sorts of people and that includes men."

"Watch who you talk to and keep your distance."

She laughed.

He watched her soberly. That caused her to hesitate a tad.

She asked carefully, "Are you going to put me in a bottle?"

Frank considered. "It would be tempting to do that, but I suppose you would like to grocery shop and visit your friends and play bridge?"

Geri tilted her head as she considered, and then she nodded.

He said, "You'll tend to do whatever you want."

Geri raised her eyebrows, and then she just waited for...whatever.

Frank sighed. "It's gonna be difficult."

"What is?" she asked with interest.

"Trying to make you behave."

She tilted her chin up and said, "I do as I choose."

"Oh, hell. One of those." He was disgusted.

But she didn't flip around and go inside her place and slam the door. Her stance simply challenged.

Frank said, "You're going to be just like my mother and try to make me into a man who'll just listen."

Geri nodded. "Okay."

"I *knew* it!"

She told him, "You can discuss this with your mother and daddy. It's late. You need some sleep. Good night." And she came to him and hugged him and kissed him, but not enough. Then she went into her apartment and closed the door.

Frank stood there in shock. He hadn't had enough! She'd been too fast! He rubbed his chest. He couldn't close his mouth but breathed through it. He felt very odd. And he had to drive his brother's pitifully stupid automobile back to his house.

And it was *his* house. The rest of the family used it, but it was Frank's. He'd completed paying the mortgage.

Frank managed to get down the steps. He was careful, paying attention to his feet, and he managed. Women were a terrible burden, he thought. They rattle a man right out of his bones.

He needed to get home and deal with his brother. If John was there, Frank would probably kill him. Naw. His mother would be horrified.

The car throbbed when Frank turned the key. It waggled the entire automobile. It was eager and ready to do just about anything! It was scary. Only his brother thought of the car as being his. Not that the car owned him, but his brother owned the car!

If the car throbbed when the key turned, the driver, whoever he was, had to put on the brake to keep the damn car safe for people on the road.

Why in the world did his brother drive such a car?

It was a challenge to drive home. Frank had to keep on the brake so the cops didn't quarrel with him. He knew exactly what to do. He went home through the alleys.

When Frank arrived home, John was in the swing, waiting for his car to be returned. He smiled as Frank turned carefully into the yard. He waited until the engine was off, then he went over and looked at the car. "Still good." He smiled.

Frank said, "Driving it was an adventure. One that I have no interest in redoing. Why in the world do you endure this automobile?"

John told him with a smile, "She's a jewel."

Frank mentioned, "I suppose it takes all kinds. I've heard that, but I didn't understand it at all until I realized this is *your* car!"

"Yep."

"John, you should consider this junk heap more closely."

John grinned. "Yeah."

Frank told him earnestly, "Keep it somewhere else. I'd hate for the younger boys to die trying to drive the damn thing."

"Right. Did you get the Queen back in her place?"

"Yeah."

"She's magic."

Frank slid his eyes over his brother and said, "Back off."

"Yes, sir." But John smiled, so amused.

Frank said, "I mean it. I'm bigger and older."

"Yeah."

"Thank you for allowing me the adventure of using this automobile. You ought to junk it."

"Not yet."

"If you ever take a real female along in that car, you are ruthless."

John blinked and became serious as he watched his big brother.

Frank asked, "You hear me?"

"Yeah. I beg your pardon."

"I forgive you. Get it fixed or exchange it. Hear me?"

"I'm woggled."

"You'll be dead if you try driving that rattletrap around anymore. Hasn't Dad or Mama spoken to you?"

"Often. I thought they were just being parents."

"No, they understand automobiles. This one is deadly. Get it over a cliff so's nobody else can be hurt by it."

"Wow. That bad?"

"Yes!"

John slitted his eyes as he considered, and he asked, "Who can I sell it to?"

"Trash it. You don't want to be the man who gives that car to somebody else. Pay attention."

"Yes."

Frank told his brother, "Don't be flippant. I'm serious."

John was earnest. "I said I would! That was yes."

"Do it."

John explained, "I have to sell it so's I can get another car."

"Tell the buyer why you have to give it up. Tell him who you are and what the car does. It could be that a man would like it for a contest of cars."

"Yeah?"

Frank said, "Yes! Listen. Hear. I'm not kidding. The car is no good. Get rid of it."

John sighed. "I can't tell you how much money I've put in that car. I've bought a lot of things to make it run."

Frank nodded. "Now's the time to get those back and let the mess go over a cliff."

"What cliff?"

"That's a joke."

"My…car."

Frank smiled. "It'll be different when you get a better one."

John sighed.

Frank shook his head. "Don't believe for one minute that this mess of a stinky car was anything you actually wanted."

John replied, "I have to give it up."

"What if it was a woman?"

John considered. He moved his head. Then he took several steps. He said, "I hadn't thought of it thataway. I believe it is time to get rid of this automobile. I'll look for something else."

"Want some company?"

John tilted his head and considered his older brother. He smiled and said, "That would be nice."

Geri joined Frank and John in the new car search. She was interested and alert. She made no comments but she did view John's car with some disgust.

John was shocked and said to her, "That's my car."

She said, "Trade it in...although I don't believe you'd get anyone interested in taking any of it. Take out the good pieces that—"

John said, "I know."

"Good! That'll get you started."

Geri and Frank smiled at each other in triumph. They felt they had John's complete understanding. She asked John, "Need us?"

John looked at her and asked, "Wanna help?"

She laughed. "I'll pass."

So John asked his big brother, "Wanna help?"

And Frank said, "Yes."

The very minute he'd said that, Geri gasped. She looked at Frank as if he had horns coming out of his head. She asked, "You're willing to help him?"

"Yeah."

She told Frank soberly, "I have other things for you to do."

John was watching her seriously. He told her, "This comes first."

Geri was shocked. She tilted her head. She was furious, but few people would realize it. She said to Frank, "Well, I'll see you in a couple of weeks or so." And she smiled, but her eyes were not amused.

John told her, "I understand."

Frank was less compassionate. He said, "See you" and lifted his hand in a goodbye motion.

There are simply things a man must do. And in this, Frank had to back his brother and encourage him in a way that John would understand what he had to do. He needed to have a car that didn't smother him with piled-up fumes.

Either John would learn to keep a good car, or he would be asphyxiated.

Frank was trying to guide his brother into something he could understand—when he could work on something, and when he was being foolish.

It was important that Geri understand. It

might take Frank's time as he helped with the car. But Frank needed to try. For his brother.

Geri smiled at Frank, realization dawning. He'd been so involved in his brother's problem of a rotten car that she hadn't realized what Frank was trying. She was so proud of him. She asked, ''Is there anything I can do?'' But she didn't ask his brother, she asked Frank.

Frank went to her and took her into his arms to hold her. His brother John was shocked. But he didn't say anything until Geri had left to go home. Then John said, ''Wow.''

And Frank said, ''Shhhh. I'm trying to breathe.''

It was probably about two weeks later that Frank and John finished the mess with the car. They tidied it up and got rid of the things they no longer needed. Then the two males went to find another car for John. Their daddy and Geri went along.

The two brothers looked and discussed and considered. And they were courteous enough to listen to their father. They thought he was too old to give them any advice. But they found he knew exactly what he was talking about.

Probably the most interested one around was Geri. She didn't direct, but she listened. If there was something that didn't seem right, she questioned it.

It was during that time that Frank's daddy understood that Geri knew all about cars. So he said to her, "How come you know so much about cars?"

Without gasping or even looking at Frank's daddy, she told him, "I watched *my* daddy."

"Ahhhhh."

So she asked Frank's daddy, "How come you're interested? Or surprised?"

"I just wondered how come you knew so much about cars. You've helped them by asking questions a couple of times without ever allowing either of those boys to know what you'd done. You're crafty and clever."

"I watched my daddy work on his own car because he drove it in races."

"Ahhhh."

Geri smiled at Frank's daddy. That was when they became friends. They understood each other.

Nine

Over the weeks Geri kept track of Frank. And she became very curious about him. She liked how he looked and how he walked and how he smiled.

For her, truly falling in love had been gradual. But she finally decided that Frank just might be what she needed as a husband. The father of her children.

After an especially tough day at a job site, Frank stopped by Geri's long enough to tell her that she was priceless.

She licked her lips to keep the smile from blooming.

His eyes laughed, but he was too tired to do anything else. Frank kissed Geri, but he was so damp and dirty from what all he'd done that day.

Geri told him softly, "You are a love."

Frank laughed softly in his throat and his eyes watched her. He was too tired to— Well, he could be persuaded.

And she said, "I'll see you another time. You stink."

Frank was shocked by that! He said, "That's honest sweat!"

"I know."

He said, "I'm so tired. Can you take me home? I don't have any clothes at your place—"

Geri told him, "Of course not. I'll take you to your house. You can sleep there."

"Oh."

So Geri did take Frank home. Along the way she allowed him to kiss her. But then she said, "You need a shower."

He considered the distance to the shower,

and the time it took to walk into a bathroom and take a shower. He said, "I think I can."

So Geri helped Frank to disrobe. He watched her with red eyes of tiredness and said, "I think I can."

"The Little Engine That Could?"

"Hush. I'm serious."

"Of course."

Geri stripped Frank down and helped him into the shower. Then she went into the bedroom and pulled back the covers on the bed.

She went back into the bathroom, having knocked and receiving no reply. Frank was leaning against the wall of the shower, half asleep. She stripped and got into the shower to wash him. He didn't lift a finger. He stood silently, his eyes serious.

Geri was gentle and kind. She washed his magnificent body slowly, memorizing every detail. His sex was extremely excited.

When she finished bathing him, she turned off the water, then she lifted his feet one at a time and got him out of the shower. She dried him. Then she led Frank into his bedroom.

He said, "Good..."

Geri ignored him. She put him into bed and covered him.

He told her, "In a minute."

She did not reply. She straightened the covers over him. She turned the coolness lower. Then she stood naked and looked at her love.

He was out.

Geri smiled at him. She knew he was exhausted. Over the past weeks he'd given a lot of his time to his brother. She thought he was a wonderful brother to his brother.

She put on her abandoned clothing and quietly went out of his apartment, making sure the door was locked. Then she left.

She went back to her apartment building, then to the third floor. No one was anywhere around. Of course, the watchful teams were. They never said a word, but they allowed her to see them and know they were there.

Geri lifted a hand to show them she'd seen them, and they smiled at her. They never spoke.

She went into her apartment, took off her clothes, dried her hair and went to bed.

The next morning, Geri had breakfast, then considered calling Frank to see if he was all right. She decided she'd go to his house and see for herself.

She looked at her watch and saw that it wasn't yet time for him to go to work. If she hurried, she'd still be able to see him. She could get into bed with him and be…rash.

Yes.

When she arrived at his house, Frank opened the door and was shocked to find her there that early. He asked immediately, "What's wrong?"

She told him, "Are you all right?"

"Yeah. What's happened? How come you're here this early?"

She said, "I rushed over here this early so that I could see you again."

He smiled and said, "Ahhh. Kiss me."

And Frank reached for her.

She allowed him to kiss her and he hugged her so nicely. He said, "You're so soft."

That woggled her, but it was a special feeling.

Eventually she watched as Frank went to his automobile and left to go to work.

He was gone.

She did all she was supposed to during that day, and waited with tolerance until Frank came home that night. He was tired. He'd worked hard again.

Geri looked at the exhausted man before her, who was her love. She was careful and watched and waited for Frank to hug her. She was curious what he would do.

Frank put a hand in her hair and wobbled her head. He grinned at her. He leaned over and kissed her. He told her she was so sweet that he just melted when she was there by him. He told her he loved her.

Geri was mush.

Frank held her to him and she smiled. Then her eyes popped open and she realized he was being rash! He groaned and held her close to him. He told her, "I love you."

How many women had he loved? She was silent.

He suffered and held her so sweetly. His

voice was gentle when he said, "You're supposed to tell me that you love me."

She said a stilted, "Yeah."

He laughed so softly. It was wicked! How come he knew how to do that? Who else did he make those sounds to?

He kissed her, and her head seemed to float off.

She was engrossed in figuring how her head would get back to her. She blinked. Now if her head was floating off and away, how come she could blink?

She looked at him. Her head was gone, off somewhere, but her eyes could look at him! How amazing! She put her hands up to see if her head *was* gone, but it was there. That didn't make sense.

In all that time, she hadn't really considered him. Frank was tired. He was sweaty. He needed to take a shower and sleep. She said, "I'll fix the bed for you."

His face showed concern. He said, "I'm not sure—"

"You'll sleep here. I'll see to it that no one bothers you."

His eyes were stark and very serious. He put a hand up to his cheek and said, "I need a shave."

She laughed softly. "No. You'll just sleep. The sheets are clean. You can be alone and snore!" She laughed over that.

He was totally blank. She wouldn't be there? She was letting him...*sleep?* He was silent, watching her. Or was she going to allow him to make love to her?

Could he? He was exhausted. He needed some time. She was so fragile. She was perfect. He'd tried to get close to her, but it had never been the right time.

Was she going to let him get close now? Later? Could he?

And she said, "You need a shower so you'll rest better."

He looked at her. Rest better? Or was it the clean sheets that she wanted to save from his sweat and grime?

Frank told her, "If you don't hear from me and the shower is still on, come wake me and get me to bed."

Geri smiled. "Okay."

She had blushed. When had he ever seen a woman blush? He was woggled. She turned him so that he'd go into the shower, and he did do that. She mentioned he ought to remove his dirty clothes and go into the shower naked.

That sounded logical. He rubbed his face and yawned hugely.

She unbuttoned his shirt and undid his trousers. She bent down and released his shoes and pulled off his socks.

He watched Geri's gentle actions with interest. And he pondered being with her as he watched Geri pull back the blankets and sheet, getting the bed ready to be used.

But he watched her with dead tired eyes and wondered if tonight they would make love. Would he survive the time, or would he fall asleep on top of her?

He asked his guardian to help him. And he went to the shower by paying close attention and by putting one foot in front of the other.

Geri stripped and got into the shower to find Frank leaning against the wall again. She washed him as she had once before. He loved it but he didn't—couldn't—open his eyes.

He told her, "Your body is luring me."

She said, "Hush."

She finished washing him and turned off the water. His breathing was deep and he was standing there, nearly asleep.

She dried him with towels and took him into the bedroom and sat him down on the sheets. She laid him flat with his head on the pillow, and then she lifted his legs up and slid them onto the bed. It was not easily done at first, but then he seemed to realize what she was doing and helped.

Geri fixed the blankets. She heard his deep breath. He was already sleeping. She moved him just a tad so that he could be more comfortable. He allowed that. She put him on his side so he wouldn't snore so loudly. He allowed that without any problem at all.

Then she stood, watching Frank sleep. He wasn't of the kind that all the rest of the family chose, but Frank was the man *she* wanted. He was a jewel. Did he know that?

She did.

Ten

How strange for Geri Jones to lure a man into her apartment and allow him to sleep there. It was rash of her. There were people around in the apartments who would know by evening—when they got back home—that Frank was with her, and those around Geri's apartment would listen to hear any conversation between the two.

For now there were no comments. There were only the rumbles of breathing as he slept.

Think of her longing for a sleeping man. She did not get into the bed. But she put her hands on her breasts and groaned. She suffered knowing such a man was so close.

She called in to her office and said she was not well, and she'd stay at her place for the day. Now that wasn't so. But the woman who took the calls offered that someone would come out and see to it that she was safe and had food.

Geri was quick in replying that she did not need any help. She just could not come to work that day. She had food. She would be in touch.

And she hung up the phone.

Frank was sleeping and his snore was very nice. It was soft. He was there. She could go and stand and watch him. She liked it that he was in her bed.

How shocking.

She smiled.

She reluctantly left the house and got her car out from the garage below, and she went to the grocery and bought all sorts of things that he could eat. She had fruit and she had foods that he liked. She took it all home and stuffed it into the refrigerator. It had been close to bare. How strange to open the door and see all that stuff! She smiled.

She smiled at everything! What was the purpose of having a man worn-out tired if she couldn't have him with her?

She came to the door of the bedroom and watched him sleep. Now, why would anybody stand around and watch a man sleep? She ought to just leave him alone!

Baloney.

She went into the kitchen and cleaned until it sparkled outrageously. Then she made a cake—but could he like pie? So she made one of those, too. The cake was white with white icing, elegant and quite pompous. The pie was pecan with brown sugar. Her daddy loved that. So another man could.

Geri was appalled at how much food she'd gotten, but it was all so perfect that she couldn't abandon any of it.

It was for Frank.

All of it.

She went to the bedroom door and looked at him yet again, and she knew he would love that food.

It would take him about a month to make a dent in what all she'd brought home from the grocery. She laughed silently.

How can a woman be so careless and foolish? Easy. She smiled. He could have whatever he wanted.

That included *her!*

She walked around with the feather duster and paid no real attention to the fact that she was tidying the house—for him.

She went through a stack of cookbooks on what to make, and she thought she really ought to take the books into his room, waken him, and show him what all he could have for supper.

She laughed again. He wouldn't know. He'd probably ask for something she'd have to go to some saloon and buy there.

Men are strange.

But God didn't give women any other replacement for men. Men are odd, no question about it, but they were so interesting!

Geri moved around all day. She tidied things and brought in flowers and she had all that stuff from the grocery. She was ready for Frank to wake up and see it all.

He slept.

She whistled. She hummed. She did all sorts of things. She tidied his bed *too* many times, but he slept like a man who was exhausted.

He'd be up all night....

Well, okay. She could handle that.

So she went to the guest room and slept like a log. She finally wakened and couldn't remember why in the world she'd chosen to move into that stark room—then she remembered!

She slid out of bed and tiptoed to the door of her room. There he was!

Asleep. In *her* bed. That was where he belonged. Not in the guest room. No. She went in and leaned over him as he belched.

She straightened quickly and looked at him

with some shock. He'd belched? Men did that? How shocking. She frowned at Frank. Belched?

She'd fed him quite a lot of food before she'd gone to bed. He'd been sleepy but tolerant.

He'd been kind to her urging him to eat. He'd done that because she had insisted.

He wasn't hungry then. And she had that mound of food that she expected him to eat! The poor man. She would see what he wanted.

She smiled. He wanted *her*.

Yes.

Well, she just might find a way for him to have her. She would see. She knew how tired he was. That exhaustion should be past— soon now. He'd open his eyes and grin at her.

He coughed.

That startled her and she smiled as she expected him to waken fully and look at her and smile.

He did not. He turned over so that his face was to the wall and the bedclothes were bunched against his stomach.

Should she straighten him out? Should she straighten out the bedclothes? Or should she leave him be?

She was uncertain. Then she realized that he'd probably never had any woman pawing at him or moving him around or hanging over him. He was grown.

She reluctantly left the room and began to tidy up the already neat house. She then went into the kitchen and made two more pies.

Geri knew that was outrageous. So she took the pies over to her friends and left them at their doors. They were mostly for the men because women don't really like that much pie when they are having trouble with weight.

She returned home and went directly to her bedroom. She looked at Frank. He was gorgeous. He was still asleep.

Frank had stuck with his brother and guided him until they were both exhausted. John had a good brother. He probably knew it already.

Moving about in the bedroom and watching Frank sleep, Geri's mind went in all directions, and Frank was in the middle of it all. She smiled.

She was very pleased that Frank was there in her bed. The only problem that she could see in him was his last name. Scheblocki was a hell of a name. What woman named Jones wanted to latch onto a name like…Scheblocki.

How could she have become involved with a man who had a name like that? She'd tolerated him having such a name because she had figured she wouldn't get snared by him!

Good gravy.

She frowned. She looked at him and thought what a dunce she was to get involved with a man whose name was Scheblocki.

Now what was she to do about that? Have *him* change *his* name to…Jones? Well, why not?

What if they—hopefully—had children and the children had to tackle the name of Scheblocki. Think of a kid in school coping with a name like that!

Women ought to pay attention to what men

have as names! If they found that out before they became involved with a man, it might help. Why wasn't Geri paying better attention?

Why couldn't his name be Smith, or Butler, or James, or Grant, or Keeper, or something simple?

Becoming Mrs. Scheblocki was too much for Geri to cope with. She'd stop this whole entire thing, wave goodbye to this person with that name and return to her safe single life.

Frank woke up to find that Geri wasn't anywhere around.

The bed was perfect. He loved the bed. It was hers. He lay there, stretched out and smiled. She'd probably want all of her side. He was in the middle and he was sprawled out so that he'd taken up most of the bed.

He cleared his throat. That was better than calling her to come to him. He was hungry for her. To have her with him in bed! Wow! He'd convince her to come to him—and to make love with him. She was probably slaving away in the kitchen. He was hungry for food. He was hungry for her, too, but he wanted to see what all she'd feed him this time. He was starving again.

He cleared his throat again.

She didn't come to him.

He yawned and made noises. If she was anywhere around, she would come to him and see if he was all right.

He'd allow her to gradually realize he was okay. He'd stretch and yawn and then she would come! And he'd say, ''You're here!'' as if he was in *his* room, and she had come to *him*.

She was not there.

That offended him somewhat because she wasn't any more alert than someone who wasn't interested.

He called out, ''Geri?''

There was no reply.

Frank finally got out of the bed and walked into the bathroom and was noisy closing the door and opening the john.

He washed his hands and face and expected

her to come into the bathroom anytime. She did not.

He opened the bathroom door and leaned against the doorjamb. He called, "Geri?"

There was silence.

The air popped, it was so still. He found he could walk somewhat, and he looked around at her apartment. It was empty. Well, there was furniture and things, but no other person. She was gone.

Had she gone down to the office for her mail? Or was she getting him something to eat at the grocery store?

He went into the kitchen and looked in the stuffed refrigerator and smiled.

She was going to feed him! Hot dog.

He hurried back to bed so that she wouldn't find him roaming around and looking at things. He was recovered, but he wouldn't allow her to know that right away. She could take care of him for a couple of days. He smiled and got back into bed.

But—

He really didn't want to be in bed. He was

restless and wanted out. So he put on a robe and went into the living room and turned on the TV.

Frank watched TV and waited for Geri to come back from wherever she'd had to go. From the looks of the refrigerator, it wouldn't be another trip to the grocery store. Frank grinned. She loved him.

The phone rang and he got up to answer it. It was Geri. She said, ''I hear you're up. Go on home. I'll not be back tonight. I'm involved otherwise. Take care.'' And just like that, she hung up the phone and had broken the contact!

Frank was stunned.

So she wasn't going to be coming back that night? And there was all that food in the refrigerator? Why had she brought home all that food and then skipped out!

So Frank sat down and ignored the TV and thought. Geri must have decided he was pulling a joke on her and just left.

Well, that wasn't *exactly* what he'd done. He'd just come back the second night and managed to be an exhausted man who needed help. And he had slept! He'd needed the rest. He was okay now, but he hadn't been faking the fact that he'd needed rest.

So she was going to be gone and he could run along home. Frank considered. There was all that food, and he'd just use it. And he'd use her house and just wait until she got back. She would need her clothes.

So he arranged the front door so that no one could possibly get in. And he made some calls to his mother and to his friends. He told them rather casually where he was and what he was doing there. He allowed them to decide exactly what all he was up to.

Then he turned on the TV and collected the evening newspaper. He read the paper and listened to the television. And he ate supper. He had some of everything she'd put into the refrigerator. He even tasted those things that were not in the freezer or refrigerator. And he watched TV while he did all that.

He was in his pajamas and he needed a shave. He could rub his chin and feel all the whiskers. He'd just wait until Geri came back and he would rub her face!

It was two days later when Geri came home. She was startled to see Frank there. His whiskers were longer. He was fragile. He said, "Where've you been? The cops are looking for you. We figured you were hijacked or stolen."

Geri was indignant. She said, "I told you to go on home!"

"Yeah, that's just like some guy that's taken you off somewhere."

"No. I called and told you that you were to leave here."

"I was too fragile."

His saying that made her hostile as all get out. She said, "There's nothing wrong with you. You're rested up and you can leave."

He told her, "You love me."

She huffed. She said, "You're to go home to your family and leave me be."

"What caused you to change? You loved me two days ago. What happened? Are you coping with menstruation?"

That made her even more mad. She told him, "No!"

He said, "Well, I'm not leaving here until you tell me what's the matter."

"Nothing. It is time for you to leave."

"Nope. I want to know how come you got all on a high horse and decided you didn't want to see me anymore. I'll move out of your room and take the other one. You have to convince me why you want me gone. You'd regret it if you lost me."

Geri lifted her hands and exclaimed, "Good gravy!"

"Gravy? You like it? I'm especially good at gravy. Shall I show you what we'll have for supper? It's ready."

Geri couldn't get rid of him. He was *there* when he wasn't at work. He fixed the meals and talked on the phone and watched TV and vacuumed the house. It had never been so pristine.

Whenever anyone came to the door, Frank got there before she did and he told her several times, "This is a man's job. It could be some leech."

He'd open the door and the woman would laugh and say, "Is it okay if I come in now?"

He'd grin and say, "We were waiting for you."

And the woman would melt. She'd talk to Geri, but she'd slide her eyes over to Frank. She would giggle and blush and she'd say to Geri, "You lucky woman!"

What was Geri to reply? She was silent. She had seen to it that Frank was there, and now there was no getting rid of him!

He cooked. He did very well. She would come home from work, tired, hot and hostile.

He would have lemonade cold and ready. He would have supper ready. He would ask her how the day went.

She would look at him with hostility.

Finally he told her kindly, "As soon as I have the chance, I'll be gone."

So that night, Geri lay in her locked room and considered Frank leaving her. She lay awake and serious. She figured that he was about what she needed as a husband. He was wonderfully kind and a good cook. He would

be the perfect father for their children. She
probably ought to test him out…first.

She told him, "I've accepted you."

Frank turned his head in shock and asked,
"Just what sort of thing do you have in
mind?"

She looked at him without any slyness at
all and told him, "I've decided I want children. You're physically—hush—in good
health—be quiet—and I believe I'll just use
you—"

He put his hand on his chest and said,
"What in this world are you talking about?"

And she said, "I want a baby. You're—
You're physically all right."

He looked down as he told her, "You'll
have to coax me."

She breathed. Her lips were tight; she did
not allow herself to say anything.

So he glanced at her and finally said, "I'll
see."

She asked, "What is it that you will want
to see?"

"If I can tolerate your sex advance." He

tilted his head and looked at her, but he did not laugh. "You need to marry me."

She became indignant, then realized there wasn't any other man she would allow to be close to her. Frank was what she'd counted on. What she needed. She said, "I want a boy."

"She could be a girl."

That boggled her. "I hadn't thought of that."

"We could see. We'll try it the first time, and if it's a girl, we'll slide in a boy."

"You're going to stay around all that time?"

"This is nice. I like it here. I have some savings. I'll take care of us."

She asked, "Why would you be here when I'm the one who is pregnant?"

He said, "We'll see."

So she asked, "Why are you going to be here 'to see.'"

"It's half my kid."

"And you feel you need to be involved with this? All you have to do is help me get pregnant."

"We ought to get married. You don't want our kid not to know his daddy."

She watched him soberly. "You'd stay home with the children?"

"I thought maybe you would. You'd know them better and I could support you."

She was shocked. "Why would you do that?"

So he told her, "I've loved you forever. And I will yet. I've wanted to marry you for a long, long time."

"Do you want a child?"

"Either kind will be fine."

She asked him seriously, "I do want children."

He told her, "When you want them, I want to help you get them. You'd be a wonderful mother. Our families will spoil these kids rotten and we'll have to be sure they're solid."

"How do we do that?"

He laughed. "We spoil them rotten?"

And she said, "Surely not."

His laugh was gentle and his eyes were on her. He watched her with such pleasure. Her eyes were alive. She was intense.

He shivered as he watched her. Geri noticed that. She licked her lips and the smile just went right on that way, and her eyes were very alert.

That was probably how Frank knew what was happening inside her because he was so intent on watching her. His body was rigid, he was so caught by her!

Men have trouble breathing around a woman. They believe they are gentle and careful.

Sure.

They watch the female with such intensity that they aren't aware of how they appear to the woman. But Geri didn't run. She smiled at Frank. She was woggled by him. He was so…male. He had been all along. That was why she'd kept him close to her without seeming to.

He knew.

They collapsed together and kissed passionately! They would have thought they were the first to ever do anything like that between two people of different sexes. When

Geri was ready, Frank slid in his sex and claimed her as his own. With every kiss, every thrust, Frank showed her the depth of his love. A love she shared. A love she knew would last forever.

Epilogue

Frank showed Geri how easy it was for a man to get a woman pregnant. It took only three months after they were married until she was finally with child. He told her, "Well, I wasn't sure that was how it was done. I'm a novice. I've never tried this getting kids as yet. What fun!"

She laughed.

So they had a girl. She was just darling and they were woggled over her. Next they had a boy and he was excellent. Before too long he took over taking care of his older sister. Then Geri and Frank gave him a brother who was younger. And after that, it was another boy and then a girl.

By then, Frank said, "I believe that's enough."

Geri commented, "But they're so different! They're so interesting! I get so I'm curious about the next one."

"I suppose we can try...one more. If it's twins, I'll be hostile."

And she said with a lifted nose, "How foolish."

So they had triplets that last time. Neither of them got over that last bunch of three girls. They truly woggled them. And Frank and Geri were more careful than they'd ever been after the triplets' birth.

Frank grinned as he entered his wife and said, "I've gotcha. You're piled around with kids and you won't dare to leave me."

She watched him. And she gradually laughed. She said, "You wonderful fool. Don't you know I could never leave you?"

"I love you."

"I love you." And she did. She'd never been so happy as when she became Mrs. Scheblocki. A decision—a name—she'd never regretted.

* * * * *

Don't miss Lass Small's next Desire,
A TEXAN COMES COURTING,
a continuation of The Keepers of Texas
available in January 2000.

THE FORTUNES OF TEXAS

*Membership in this family has
its privileges…and its price.
But what a fortune can't buy,
a true-bred Texas love is sure to bring!*

Coming in November 1999…

Expecting…
In Texas
by

MARIE
FERRARELLA

Wrangler Cruz Perez's night of passion with Savannah Clark
had left the beauty pregnant with his child. Cruz's cowboy
code of honor demanded he do right by the expectant
mother, but could he convince Savannah—and himself—
that his offer of marriage was inspired by true love?

THE FORTUNES OF TEXAS continues with
A Willing Wife by Jackie Merritt,
available in December 1999 from
Silhouette Books.

Available at your favorite retail outlet.

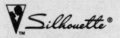

Silhouette®

PSFOT3

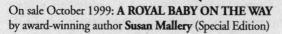
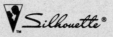

In December 1999
three spectacular authors invite you to share the
romance of the season as three special gifts are

Delivered by Christmas

A heartwarming holiday anthology featuring

BLUEBIRD WINTER
by *New York Times* bestselling author
Linda Howard

A baby is about to be born on the side of the road. The single
mother's only hope rests in the strong arms of a dashing doctor....

And two brand-new stories:

THE GIFT OF JOY
by national bestselling author **Joan Hohl**

A bride was not what a Texas-Ranger-turned-rancher was
expecting for the holidays. Will his quest for a home lead to love?

A CHRISTMAS TO TREASURE
by award-winning author **Sandra Steffen**

A daddy is all two children want for Christmas. And the
handsome man upstairs may be just the hero their mommy needs!

*Give yourself the gift of romance in
this special holiday collection!*

Available at your favorite retail outlet.

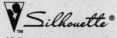

Visit us at www.romance.net   PSDBC

SILHOUETTE® Desire®

COMING NEXT MONTH

#1249 HEART OF TEXAS—Mary Lynn Baxter
Man of the Month 10th Anniversary
Businessman Clark Garrison had come home to River Oaks for
one purpose—to make a profit. But that was before he met
Dr. Sara Wilson...and realized his profit would be her loss.
Would Sara still want to be his partner in life once the truth
was revealed?

#1250 SECRET AGENT DAD—Metsy Hingle
Texas Cattleman's Club
Widow Josie Walter had never wanted to get close to another
man again, but she couldn't help believing in happily-ever-after
when handsome amnesiac Blake Hunt landed on her doorstep—
with four-month-old twins. But once regained, would Blake's
memory include a knowledge of the love they'd shared?

#1251 THE BRIDE-IN-LAW—Dixie Browning
His father had eloped! And now Tucker Dennis was faced with
the bride's younger niece, Annie Summers. Annie only wanted
her aunt's happiness, but when she met Tucker, she couldn't help
but wonder if marrying him would make *her* dreams come true.

#1252 A DOCTOR IN HER STOCKING—Elizabeth Bevarly
From Here to Maternity
He had promised to do a good deed before the end of the day,
and Dr. Reed Atchinson had decided that helping pregnant
Mindy Harmon was going to be that good deed. The stubborn
beauty had refused his offer of a home for the holidays—but
would she refuse his heart?

#1253 THE DADDY SEARCH—Shawna Delacorte
Lexi Parker was determined to track down her nephew's father.
But the man her sister said was responsible was rancher
Nick Clayton—a man Lexi fell in love with at first sight. Would
Nick's passion for her disappear once he found out why she was
on his ranch?

#1254 SAIL AWAY—Kathleen Korbel
Piracy on the high seas left Ethan Campbell on the run—and in
the debt of his rescuer, Lilly Kokoa. But once—*if*—they survived,
would Ethan's passion for Lilly endure the test of time?